CUTTHROAT

SUTTON CAPITAL INTRIGUE SERIES BOOK 1

LORI RYAN

The Sutton Capital Series

Legal Ease

Penalty Clause

The Baker's Bodyguard (A Sutton Capital Series Novella)

Negotiation Tactics

The Billionaire's Suite Dreams

The Baker, the Bodyguard, and the Wedding Bell Blues (A Sutton Capital Series Novella)

Her SEALed Fate

The Sutton Capital Series Boxed Set (Books One Through Four)

The Sutton Capital Series Boxed Set (Books Five Through Seven)

Sutton Capital Intrigue

Cutthroat

Cut and Run

Cut to the Chase

Sutton Capital On the Line Series

Pure Vengeance

Latent Danger

Wicked Justice

ISBN: 978-1-941149-56-0

ACKNOWLEDGMENTS

As always, I am indebted to several friends and experts who took the time to answer my questions and share their expertise. The generosity of those I've reached out to always amazes me. I couldn't write these books without the help of a lot of people!

Any errors or changes due to creative license are my own.

I'd like to thank Meredith Elkins, D. P. Lyle, Jon and Shari Bartholomew, and Garry Rodgers for your expertise. The way you take time out of your day to help me is humbling.

Redmond Ramos, thank you for answering all of my questions and sharing your experiences, but also for being such an inspiration!

Scott Silverii, I can't thank you enough for answering my endless texts and emails. Maybe someday, I'll run out of questions. But probably not.

Thank you Karen Henderson, Zebbie Starnes, and Sara Smith for your beta reading and proofing assistance. You guys just rock!

Thank you to Jessie Winter for editing and meeting my timeline again.

Melanie, you have no idea how happy I am to have found you! Brainstorming with you makes all the difference. I'm sorry I made you read this one so many times.

Ehlane and Cathy, I just love you guys.

All right, now I'm getting all teary-eyed. This has to stop. Go read the book, and know it was written by a village!

To those who don't always have a voice in this world.

CHAPTER 1

EGGS FRYING in butter was probably his favorite smell in the world.

Jaxon Ray Cutter flipped the eggs in the frying pan, the scent of butter filling the kitchen. The sound of gruff laughter behind him joined the pop and sizzle coming from the pan.

"Still makes me laugh every time I see it." Leo Kent crossed the small space of the studio apartment and dropped into a chair.

Jax shot him a grin over his shoulder. He knew what his friend was referring to. It was what had started the unlikely friendship in the first place. A tattoo he'd gotten soon after losing part of his leg below the knee.

The black tattoo on his right calf was designed to look like somebody had written on his leg in magic marker. The word *POSER* hovered over an arrow that pointed to the prosthesis on his left leg. The tattoo was a prime example of Jax's wry sense of humor.

It wasn't the only tattoo to grace his skin. He had tribal

work from the top of his shoulder down most of one arm, and a few other pieces on his back. He'd celebrated his freedom when leaving the Navy with a few pieces that required multiple hours in the chair. Although nowadays sailors could have more tattoos under looser restrictions, when he'd been in, his tattoos would have landed him in hot water.

"Always happy to be your entertainment," Jax said, turning back to the stove. It wasn't uncommon for Jax to stop by Leo's apartment after his morning run for breakfast. He wasn't sure if the older man would eat if Jax didn't swing by to be sure.

Their meeting had been a chance one, but they'd hit it off right away. When Jax had taken a break from his run two years back, Leo had spotted the tattoo and laughed so hard he almost choked. The Gulf War vet had his own prosthetic leg but didn't have the fancy tattoo to go with it.

Leo's amputation was above-the-knee, unlike Jax's below-the-knee. From what he knew, Jax should be grateful for that. There was a lot more pain and discomfort involved with wearing a prosthesis on an above-the-knee residual limb, not to mention the loss of a natural knee.

Jax slid fried eggs and buttered toast onto a plate and dropped the plate onto the table in front of Leo. He sat opposite and dug into his own meal before realizing Leo wasn't eating.

"Something wrong with your food?"

"I, uh, wanted to give you this." What looked to be six or eight twenty dollar bills, folded in half, landed on the table. Leo turned to eat like it was nothing for him to have that amount of money.

Jax knew full well it was a lot more than nothing to the man who'd been homeless only six months ago. If Leo hadn't let Jax help him pay the security deposit and a little of the rent, he'd still be living on the streets.

"What the hell is that?" Jax stared at the money. He'd known it would be hard to get Leo to take money from him, but he figured once he got him into the apartment, the man wouldn't worry so much about it. He'd never in a million years intended for Leo to pay him back.

"A man pays his debts." Leo didn't look up as he spoke. Just kept shoveling eggs in his mouth.

"You don't have a debt. And even if you did, it's not one I would ever ask you to pay."

"I'm just saying a man pays his debts that's all. I fully intend to pay you back everything you've given me."

"Not necessary," Jax said. He was starting to get pissed. "Use the money for something you need. Clothes, medical care—there has to be something."

"Nah, I got what I need. I get medical care from the clinic and what the hell do I need with more clothes? More to wash, that's all that does. What I do need is to make sure my friend is paid back."

"Where'd you get it?" *Shit.* He hadn't meant for that to come out. He had no business—no right—to question where Leo got anything.

The older man pretended the question wasn't out of line. "Turns out, when you got a place to sleep and shower, a little food in your belly, it's a lot easier to get work. I've just been picking up day work, that's all." A shrug accompanied the words. Jax could see Leo was leaving something out of that story, but he wasn't going to push it.

There was no way he'd win this fight. He picked up the money, split the pile in half and pushed one half back toward his friend. They'd have to compromise.

"You go to that happy hour last night?" Leo asked as he scowled at the money.

Now it was Jax's turn to grunt his response. He did so at the same time he cursed himself for ever mentioning the stupid Thursday after-work tradition at Sutton Capital. He liked the people he worked with, but he just wasn't ready for hanging out in a bar where he had to talk to strangers. He'd tried. It had sucked.

"You didn't, did you?"

Jax ignored the question, filling his mouth with enough toast that he couldn't speak around it. He wasn't going to talk about this. If anyone should accept the fact that he wasn't cut out to hang out with civilians, it should be Leo.

"You should make more of an effort."

Apparently not. "Why is that?"

"So you don't end up like my sorry ass, dick head." Leo never bothered to pretty up his language for Jax. "You want to end up lucky as hell to have one friend in this jackoff world? Keep it up."

"Dick head? Really?"

Leo just laughed and went back to his food, but Jax knew he would continue to pester him about it. He'd made the effort, though, just like he'd said. He tried going out for drinks with everyone after work. The only problem was, he ended up angry and annoyed more often than not. If he had to listen to one more person bitch about waiting three hours for the cable guy to come hook up their effing television, or the fact that they couldn't find the right color shoes to match an outfit (this from a guy, no less!), he'd lose his shit.

His friends at work weren't the problem. In fact, he liked the team he worked with a lot. Many of them were former military, too. Others had married former military. It was the other people they'd meet when they went out that screwed with shit. People who hadn't served just didn't get it. Didn't get how lucky they were or how freaking ungrateful they can sound at times. Didn't have the first clue what it meant to really hurt, to really need. To bleed with body, heart, and soul all at once.

Conversation stopped while they finished up their breakfast, each sipping from a cup of black coffee brewed thicker than mud. The silence wasn't a heavy or uneasy one. It just was. It was what they were used to and one of the reasons they were friends. No need for extra conversation or talk.

Leo stood and picked up the empty plates, taking them to the sink. Other people might have thought the man was a project to Jax. He was anything but that. Jax needed Leo as much as Leo needed him. When Jax separated from the Navy, he discovered he had a hard time finding people he was comfortable with. There were a few other veterans at work he got along with, but that was it. For the most part, he and civilians just didn't mix. Until Leo, he'd been going to work and going home.

He shoved his chair back and went to the other side of the small room, glancing over his shoulder to make sure Leo was still busy at the sink. He stuck the forty or so bucks he'd taken out of the pile of cash on the table into the inside pocket of the fishing vest Leo wore most days. No way in hell he was taking money from the man.

"I have to get to work soon. You need anything before I head out?" Jax crossed back to the kitchen, glancing up to see Leo hunched over the counter, the color draining from his face. "Hey, you okay?"

"Shit." He took Leo by the shoulders and steadied him as he lowered him back into the kitchen chair.

It'd been a couple of years since Jax had left his detail as a Navy Corpsman to the Marines—essentially a field medic —but his medical training still took over within an instant. He stopped the useless cursing as he checked Leo's pulse.

His friend tried to bat his hand away, grumbling that he was fine, but needed to rest.

"You're hardly fine. You look gray."

"Forgot to put my makeup on today." Leo pursed his lips and made kissing noises as he crossed his eyes at Jax. His color was coming back, but Jax still stayed close as he checked him over.

"Funny. I don't know why you haven't had a career in comedy all these years."

"You about done, Mom?" asked Leo. "I think I'll lie down and rest now, if you're done playing that Florence whatever-her-name is chick."

Jax eyed him once more, before shoving back on his heels. "Yeah, I'm done."

Jax busied himself with cleaning up the kitchen counter and putting the last evidence of the breakfast making away as Leo laid on his bed. The older man crossed his arms behind his head and closed his eyes before speaking again.

"Hey, when you take off, toss that letter in the mail for me, will you? On the counter there?"

Jax looked around and spotted the small envelope. "Sure. I'll swing by tomorrow and see if you're feeling better. Call if you need me, though, huh?"

Leo grunted a response and raised his hand. That was all the goodbye Jax was going to get. He glanced at the envelope again, reaching for his car keys. No return address. As he grabbed a pen and scribbled in Leo's name and address in the upper left corner of the envelope, he wondered briefly who Michaela Kent was. Possibilities ran through his head.

A loud snore came from the bed. Jax shook his head and left, locking the door behind him. Whoever she was, he wouldn't be getting that story out of Leo today.

* * *

Mia Kent frowned at the envelope topping the stack of mail on her desk. Its face was down, but she knew it would be addressed to Michaela Kent. And that simple fact alone told her who it was from. There wasn't a soul on the planet who called her that, except her father. In fact, the name didn't even appear on her birth certificate. Her mother had changed it when she was only seven years old.

Leaning into her desk drawer, she tugged out one of the plain white envelopes she kept in a neat stack at the back. This had become a routine. The money arrived from her father every week. No note or anything. Just a stack of cash. Why he thought it was safe to send cash through the mail, she would never know. Nor did she care. She simply opened the envelope, moved the cash into an unmarked envelope, and would drop it into the church donation box on her way home.

"Who sends things unsolicited to someone at their place of business, anyway?" She had a habit of talking to herself, and that kicked into high gear when she received these letters. "Completely unprofessional," she muttered.

Not that it mattered. She was the Office Manager at the medium sized law firm of Schuler and Koskoff. As long as she kept the office running smoothly—which she did—her bosses didn't care if she received personal calls or mail. It was the principle of it that bothered her, though.

As Mia tossed the envelope in the trash, her hand froze. A return address. Today's envelope contained a return address. And there in black and white, her father's name. *Leo Kent.*

"New Haven," she said aloud to the empty office, an odd tingling sensation running over her arms "Has he actually been in New Haven all this time?"

Not that she cared. She didn't. She was simply shocked to discover how close he'd been to her own home in Hartford, just over an hour north.

Close enough that he could have come to see her.

Could have shown up at her soccer games or high school graduation, at the very least. Or her college graduation when she'd earned that coveted BA from Trinity. The one she and her mom had worked so hard to fund?

Anger flashed in her gut and Mia shredded the envelope. Tossing the pieces in the trash. It didn't take long for her to reach back in and pull the pieces out. She smoothed the crinkled paper and taped the return address back together.

"Better." Now she could handle this problem head on, just like she always did when faced with something that wasn't working in her life. She'd go to New Haven this weekend and put an end to the letters. She'd tell Leo Kent she didn't need his money, or him.

Nick Traber poked his head in her office. "You about ready?"

Mia nodded, shoving the envelope back in her desk drawer and straightening her skirt. She'd been dating Nick for six months. There was a steadiness to him she found comforting and his blue eyes were kind. She also liked that he was taller than her own five feet eight inches.

When she'd been in college, Mia had dated a guy who

began talking about a future with her almost immediately. He felt things so strongly, he began to scare her pretty early on in their relationship. Gary Schake had very quickly shown her what it was like to be with someone who cared too much. Who felt things too hard. And when she'd tried to break things off, it had gotten ugly and more than a little scary for a while.

Things with Nick weren't like that. When she'd first seen him, her immediate thought was that he was nice looking. Brown hair, gentle brown eyes. A dimple when he smiled. He was a good looking man, but not so good looking that he'd be arrogant about it. She liked that.

Their feelings for each other had built slowly, and she liked that. They didn't have to discuss where to eat. They'd walk down to the diner on the corner while he told her about his caseload. It was what they did every time they met for lunch.

Nick was an independent lawyer who leased office space in the same building as her firm. He primarily handled trusts and estates, with some occasional real estate law thrown in.

When they got to the diner, he would order a BLT on wheat toast, hold the mayo. He'd drink unsweetened iced tea. Two of them. Mia smiled as he started telling her about something he'd done with a trust he thought would save the client money in the long run. Something about how he set it up.

She could breathe again when she was with Nick. She slipped her hand into his and he glanced her way and smiled.

"Hungry?" he asked.

"Starved," she said, as he launched into details about remainders and living wills and all the things that bored her to tears, but reminded her how steady he was. She took a deep breath and left all thoughts of her father and his unwanted money behind.

CHAPTER 2

MIA RAPPED TWICE on the door of apartment 3C and wiped her hand on her pants. She didn't know why her palms were sweating. It was simple, really.

"Tell him you don't want his money and he needs to stop contacting you," she said under her breath, aware of how it would look if people saw her talking to herself out loud. "Tell him you'll get a restraining order if he doesn't stop. Simple."

She let out a breath and looked around. The building was small. Probably only twenty apartments in the three stories. It was modest, but clean and in a better area of town than she'd thought it would be. Not upscale, but not run down and unsafe the way she'd expected. Truth be told, it was in a better neighborhood than some of the ones she and her mom had lived in over the years.

She didn't have time to process how that made her feel before the door swung open and Mia took a step back. Intense blue eyes.

This couldn't be right. A man, in his thirties, maybe late

twenties, smiled at her. He was much too young to be Leo Kent.

"Can I help you?"

She glanced down at the taped together envelope in her hands, then up again at the 3C on the side of the door frame. She was in the right place.

A son?

The hurt and insecurity of her younger years came flooding at her. Why hadn't it occurred to her that her dad could have remarried? That he had a new family? Children he had raised and still saw? Maybe even lived with?

When she was young, she'd imagined all kinds of things. That he hadn't really wanted to leave. That he was part of a top secret mission for the military, that they'd called him back into service for a job only he could do.

Another prize winner had been the amnesia theory. The one where he'd been in an accident or hit in the head trying to thwart a robbery and couldn't remember who he was. But one day, he'd walk back into her life, remembering everything. Remembering he had a little girl he loved. Remembering that he wanted her.

How had it never occurred to her to think he had a new family? That he had moved on and didn't need her.

"Miss? Are you all right?"

Now the features of the man in front of her creased in concern. He was good looking, with strong features and intense eyes. She wondered briefly if his face looked like her father's. She had only a vague memory of her dad, and honestly, the memories she did have weren't truly memories. They came from pictures. The few pictures her mom had of him. One in his uniform, and another of him holding Mia as an infant and smiling at the camera.

Did this man look like her dad? He had a chiseled face,

the kind of bone structure movie stars had. Those shockingly blue eyes watched her, waiting for a response and her stomach flipped. Something about his gaze unsettled her. Like he could see right through her. But she really couldn't say one way or the other if he looked like her dad.

He glanced at the mangled envelope she held and a smile crossed his face. "You must be Michaela. Are you here to see Leo?"

She swallowed. "I'm sorry, I have the wrong apartment." She didn't wait for a response, but she felt the man's eyes on her as she hightailed it to the stairwell and through the door.

Then she heard another voice. This one deep and gravelly from inside the apartment. She froze on the stairs, straining to hear. "Who's there, Jax?"

"I'm not exactly sure. Wrong place, I guess."

The door to the stairwell slammed shut behind Mia blocking out the rest of the conversation as she cursed herself for being stupid enough to come here. It wasn't until this moment that she realized she'd been fooling herself. She hadn't come just to tell him to leave her alone.

She'd wanted to see him. On some small level, the little girl inside her was still hoping her daddy cared about her. Still hoping for more than money sent without so much as a note or a letter. The stupid dreams of a little girl who still wanted her daddy to come home. She clamped down on the foolish tears forming and shook her head. No way would she let him tear her heart in two again.

Jax shut the door and looked back at Leo. He didn't know if he should tell Leo about the woman or not. He looked better than he had the past few days, but still a little off. And Jax didn't know what to make of the woman. Maybe he'd been wrong. He thought she was holding the envelope he'd mailed for Leo, but she certainly hadn't answered to the name. He thought maybe there'd been a look of panic in her eye when she heard it.

"Hey, Leo, who's Michaela? The woman you had me mail that letter to?"

Leo stopped mid-stride for the briefest of seconds on his way to the kitchen, only to then keep moving like nothing had happened.

"None of your concern." His friend's voice was gruff and abrupt and he didn't bother to turn and look at Jax as he spoke.

Jax understood not wanting to talk about something. They all had their shit they wouldn't talk about and he respected that. "Listen, I have to meet Logan in ten, but if you're not better Monday I'm taking you to the clinic."

Leo didn't argue, which told Jax just how bad he was feeling. He hesitated at the door. He could cancel his bike ride with Logan.

Seeing him hesitate, Leo waved him off. "I'm fine, fine."

"You call me if you start to feel worse." He pointed at Leo as he spoke. It was always a tossup which one of them was more stubborn, but come hell or high water, he was bringing Leo in if this didn't stop.

He shut the door and hit the button for the elevator. He always walked up the three flights but took the elevator down. Walking down steps seemed to make his stump ache in the socket of his prosthesis these days. He needed to get back to his prosthetist for a refit. When he'd first come back from overseas, he'd seen his prosthetist weekly, even twice a week sometimes. It took a while to get the right fit. Nowadays, though, he wasn't nearly as good about getting in there and he was paying for it with pressure sores. If he didn't watch it, his skin would break down and he'd be in for an earful when he finally showed his face in their office again.

He stopped in the parking lot and pulled out his phone, planning to call for an appointment right then. If his walking leg wasn't fitting well, he doubted his cycling one would be any better. But he didn't make the call, after all.

She was sitting in a small blue sedan, hands clamped down so hard on the steering wheel he could see the whites of her knuckles. The woman who'd come to the door. Her face looked as haunted now as it had when she'd seen him in Leo's apartment. She had what seemed like never-ending cascades of hair falling down her back and it was that girl-next-door shade of brown he'd always loved. The kind that looked a little red when the sun hit it just right.

He was pretty sure she didn't even see him as he approached the window.

"Now I know you're not okay," he called through the glass, as he bent to see through the window.

Startled eyes turned his way but he saw hurt in them as well. Jax stepped back as she floored her car in reverse and drove away.

Whoever Michaela Kent was, she was hurting.

CHAPTER 3

"SHIT, THAT LOOKS BAD." Logan winced as he spoke, and Jax had to agree.

A two-inch patch of skin where his prosthesis was rubbing the wrong way was more than sore. He should have cancelled the bike ride and gone home for some serious skin care followed by an appointment at his prosthetist. He was stupid that way sometimes.

He shrugged. "I'll go home and soak it."

"Is that supposed to happen?" Logan was a Navy SEAL and had come home with his own injuries. His weren't as obvious as Jax's amputated leg was, but they were there.

Logan had struggled with some pretty serious PTSD for a while, and he had some physical stuff that would likely lead to a great deal of pain as he aged.

They all had their shit to deal with.

"No. I haven't been getting my prosthesis re-fitted lately. My stump must have changed shape."

Logan just looked at him, brows up with that *you're dumber than a post* look the man was so good at.

Jax laughed. "Yeah, yeah, I know. I'm an idiot."

He pulled a clean, dry sock over his stump and stood on his right leg, balancing with one hand on the car, without putting his walking prosthesis back on. He'd need to drive home without it and go soak his leg.

"I'll skip work in the morning and get it taken care of." He switched to the one topic he was sure would avert Logan's focus. "How's Sam? She still insisting on going to work?"

"Yes," grumbled Logan, drawing a laugh from Jax.

"You realize she's not the only woman on the planet to keep working until the baby comes right? I mean, I get you're worried about all that sitting in front of a desk she does, and all, but—"

He cut off when Logan punched him in the shoulder, knocking him into the side of his car. He righted himself and laughed again. Logan was fun to torment when his wife was pregnant. It was beyond easy to get a rise out of the normally staid SEAL.

"She should rest."

"Yeah," Jax nodded. "The desk thing is strenuous, man. She should really rest."

"You're a riot."

"Seriously, she's got three more weeks, right?"

"Yeah." If Sam let him, Logan might take overprotective to new heights, but from what Jax had heard, their friends Jack and Chad had been pretty much the same when their wives were pregnant. Luckily, Samantha was a strong personality herself. She likely just laughed at the big guy and blew right on past him.

Jax had a flash thought, wondering if he'd be that way someday. He stopped it in its tracks. He never let his thoughts go there. For now, he was focused on putting one foot in front of the other. Well, one stump and a foot in front of the other. He'd make time for dating later.

He knew what was holding him back, and it was stupid. He had adjusted far better than some of his friends to being an amputee.

When that explosive had hit him and he'd seen the wreckage to his limb, he'd laughed. Freaking laughed. Because all he could think was, *I'm alive. I was hit and I'm still here*, like he'd gotten a rubber bullet in a game of Russian roulette.

A piece of his leg was a damned small thing to lose. He could run, bike, swim. All the shit he loved to do. He wasn't self-conscious about his prosthetic leg, and didn't care that he'd had to give up a limb during his service.

But he was self-conscious about his residual limb when it came to being with a woman. The piece of leg below his knee was twisted, the skin over it scarred. There was a little fold at the stump, like the doctors had folded the skin and tucked it up before stitching it.

When it came to adjusting to life as an amputee, there was really only one thing he hadn't done yet. And it was stupid. So stupid, he'd never even told Logan or Leo or anyone he was struggling with it.

He hadn't been with a woman yet. Sex was the one hurdle he froze up about. He didn't know why. It wasn't like he'd ever thought about his body before and worried how a woman might see him. Now, though, he absolutely did.

Stupid? Yes.

Beyond his ability to get over for the time being? Yeah. That.

So, he'd focus on work for now and figure that shit out when he grew a pair of balls. Those, thankfully, had not been hit in the explosion. Close. There was a seven-inch jagged scar next to his groin to prove how close it had been, but the wonder twins were still intact.

"Sam wants you to come for dinner someday before the baby gets here."

Jax nodded and opened his car door, holding onto the frame as he lowered himself into the seat. "Tell her I'm only coming if she swears not to go into labor while I'm there."

"You were a Corpsman. You can't handle a woman in labor, you wuss?"

"Damn right. Especially not when that woman is your wife. I'm not delivering any babies in your living room."

Now Logan winced and Jax shut the door and drove off, no doubt leaving his friend picturing his worst nightmare. He felt a twinge of guilt. Logan would likely want to camp out across the street from the hospital to be sure he could get Sam there in time. Jax should probably apologize to Sam for that one.

* * *

"So, you haven't known where he was all this time?" Nick asked, his hand resting on Mia's knee as they sat on her couch. It was movie night, but so far they hadn't put the movie in, or even ordered take out yet.

"No." Mia couldn't believe she hadn't told him all of this yet, but when she thought about it, they typically talked about work. "And when I went there, I just chickened out."

"Wait, you went there?" Nick sounded shocked, and if she wasn't mistaken, there was censure in his tone as well.

"Of course I did. I want him to stop sending me money."

"Why? Take his money. It sounds like he owes you."

Nick leaned forward and grabbed the DVD he'd brought, standing to move to the DVD player to pop it in.

She frowned as she thought about his reaction. "I don't know. I just want him to know I don't need his money." Maybe she wanted him to know she'd made something of herself. That despite not having him in her life, she and her mom had turned out just fine.

Nick sat back by her side, remote in hand. "I just don't see why you'd do that. Why invite him back into your world?" Okay, definitely censure in there.

Mia didn't really have an answer for that, but part of her bristled at the way Nick was acting. She knew Nick didn't like change all that much, but he was acting as though she was foolish for going to see her father.

No, that wasn't it. He was acting as if she were a child who needed to be told what to do.

"Why not invite him back into my world?" She wasn't sure why she was pushing the issue. Maybe she just wanted to know what was behind Nick's objections.

He shrugged. "It's just messy, that's all. You said yourself, you don't need him. So why open yourself up to be hurt by him again? Once a deadbeat, always a deadbeat."

Mia winced. She'd always tried to hide the truth about her dad from friends for just that reason. She didn't want people to know he was a deadbeat dad who'd left her and her mom. On some level, she supposed her child's mind had always seen it as a reflection on her. That she hadn't been worth sticking around for.

And if she was being fair, he wasn't a deadbeat dad. Her dad had made sure she and her mom had received his disability compensation over the years. He'd supported them. He just hadn't been there.

Nick's choice of words stung now. He'd picked at an old wound scabbed over, but not quite healed, and she wondered if he even realized how much those words could hurt her.

CHAPTER 4

"AND, SHE'S BACK." The mystery woman had returned. Jax knew the woman even from the back.

She stood poised in front of Leo's door, hand suspended as if she were trying to knock but forgot how to do it. He suspected she was Michaela Kent, the woman from the envelope, and possibly Leo's daughter, judging by her age and the shared last name. Or maybe a niece?

He stopped on the steps behind her, Leo next to him. They'd just returned from breakfast at their favorite diner after Leo had managed to convince Jax he was feeling better. With the small amount Leo had eaten at breakfast, Jax wasn't at all sure he was buying it.

The woman turned at their approach, her eyes locked on Leo. That's when Jax realized Leo was just as frozen as she'd been a moment before. He also figured out pretty quickly why she'd seemed so familiar to him. She had Leo's eyes. The chestnut brown color was a dead match to the man standing next to him.

"Everything all right, Leo?" he asked as the silence between the small group drew on.

"Jax, this is my daughter, Michaela. Michaela, a friend of mine, Jaxon Cutter."

"Mia." The woman corrected, but it wasn't with the friendly tone of someone who was communicating a nickname after an introduction. No, this was a true correction, as though the name Michaela offended her in some way.

"May we speak privately?" Her body was ramrod straight and her tone cold as ice. Leo glanced his way, but nodded and unlocked the door to the apartment, shutting it after Mia joined him.

Jax leaned against the outside wall and waited. It was stupid for him to worry, but he had a feeling this woman had the ability to cut Leo to the core. And he sure as hell wasn't about to let that happen.

* * *

"I'd like you to stop sending me money." Mia crossed her arms and resisted the urge to look around the room. To try to soak in details. To try to decipher who her father was. "I don't need it and I don't want it."

He looked older than she thought he would, the stamp of a life hard lived marked on his face in lines and wrinkles. The dark hair she remembered now peppered with gray.

"How'd you find me?" he asked.

"From your letter. The return address on the envelope." Her arms dropped to her side as understanding dawned. He hadn't written the return address. He hadn't wanted her to know where he was.

Sending money was one thing, but actually seeing her? Knowing her? Apparently he didn't want to see her any more than she wanted to see him.

The knowledge shouldn't bother her. After all, she was

here to tell him to leave her alone and stay out of her life. So why did it hurt so damned bad to know that had been his plan all along?

Her father glanced at the door and understanding seemed to dawn on his face. "Ah. He meant well." He walked to the couch and sat, and Mia noticed his leg for the first time. The man outside had an artificial limb, she realized and wondered if he was also a veteran. Maybe that was the connection between the two men.

"You didn't want to be found, did you?" She didn't know why she was pushing this. Why the hell she wanted to hear him say it.

Mia had never thought of herself as a glutton for punishment. She was independent and strong. Just like her mom was. Just like her mother had taught her to be. So why did she feel like a child begging to hear her father tell her he loved her. That he wanted her?

"It's just better this way. Better if we don't—" He didn't finish, just waved a hand as if that explained it all.

Mia nodded, feeling a painful lump in her throat. "You're right. It's better this way." She glanced around, not knowing what else to say. "I just came to tell you to stop sending money."

He nodded but didn't say anything as she walked out the door.

Mia jumped when she heard Jax speak the second she shut the door.

"If you really only wanted to tell him to stop sending money, you wouldn't have come all the way here. Twice."

She spun and saw Jax push himself away from the wall where he'd clearly heard her conversation with her dad. Her heart slammed in her chest and she didn't think it was just the startle response of him catching her off guard. The man had an intensity to him that caught and shook her. But that didn't change the anger she felt as she realized he'd listened to every humiliating second of her short talk with her dad.

"Do you always listen in on private conversations?" She couldn't believe the nerve of him. He looked wholly unapologetic as he stepped toward her, as if he had every right to listen in on her. To judge her and call her out on why she was here.

"Do you always avoid tough conversations?"

"Yes." She couldn't help but raise her chin at him. "When they involve people who have no business being involved."

Jax stepped closer but she took a step backward, needing to keep space between herself and this man.

"He's a good man. He doesn't deserve to be hurt."

Ha! What a joke. "You've got things backwards here, mister."

"Not from where I'm standing. By my count, you've come down here twice. The first time might not count because he didn't see you, but this time you got him involved and now you're running off the first time he says boo to you. Either you want him in your life or you need to walk away and not come back this time."

"He told me to leave."

"Don't you know squat about how people work?"

Mia felt like he'd slapped her. No. She guessed she wasn't very good with people. She didn't say anything and the man continued.

"He sent you away because he's hurting. If you come back, you need to be sure it's for good next time."

"Screw you." She spun and walked away. Leaving and *not* coming back was what she had in mind.

CHAPTER 5

JAX LET himself into Leo's apartment and found him sitting on the couch staring at the door. His pallor was still gray, and there was no way in hell Jax was going to take more excuses. He needed to see a doctor.

"That was pretty heavy. You okay?"

"Yeah." Leo shrugged. "She hasn't been in my life since she was three. I didn't have any hope she would be now."

Jax thought about apologizing for putting Leo's return address on the envelope, but didn't. He wasn't sure it was a bad thing for a man to see his child after all those years. He didn't know if Leo had noted it, but the woman looked like she'd made something of herself.

She had the look of someone who took great care in their appearance, even wearing a nice sweater and pressed pants on the weekend. Not exactly Jax's thing, but she looked nice. Maybe it would do Leo good to see that, to know his daughter wasn't struggling.

He picked up the worn out fishing vest Leo had dropped on the couch and tossed it at his friend. The pockets were stuffed with everything from keys to wallet to pill bottles. Leo took whatever he needed with him every-where he went.

"Come on. We're going to the clinic."

Leo didn't argue. *Hell.* That meant he felt as crappy as he looked.

Two hours later, Jax sat in the cramped waiting room of the clinic attached to New Haven's homeless shelter and scrolled through emails on his phone. He didn't usually work on a Sunday, but he didn't have anything else to do while he waited. At least not if he wanted to keep his mind off Mia Kent.

He'd stupidly been wondering if she was okay since she'd left Leo's earlier. As much as he didn't want her toying with Leo's emotions, he had seen the look on her face when she'd left. These visits were ripping her open. Even so, it was stupid for him to be worrying about a woman he didn't know.

So, he turned to work to try to keep thoughts of her at bay. It wasn't working all that well. She kept waltzing through his mind, the hurt and anger in her eyes making him want to reach out and hold her.

What the hell was that about?

Jax shook his head and brought himself back to the here and now. One wall of the waiting room held plaques thanking their donors. Jax's eyes scanned down the *Premier Donors*:

Simms Pharmaceutical

Branson Medical

Tyvek Technologies

The Victoria Tyvek Staunton Memorial Foundation.

He wondered what it took to become a *Premier Donor* and how much more than the other donors they had donated. The clinic building was clean and neat, but it was small. Every ounce of space seemed to be in use. Maybe they should ask those *Premier Donors* to pay for an addition to the building.

The waiting room was packed with people waiting to see a doctor. He guessed that's why the clinic was open seven days a week. There didn't seem to be a shortage of people who needed them. Sadly, he knew it was just the opposite. They had more people needing services than they had resources, but from what he knew this clinic was fairly well funded by private donations and volunteers.

Leo could have gone to the VA hospital, but he'd lost his trust in the military a long time ago. Connecticut had begun an enormous undertaking in the past year to bring veteran homelessness to something called functional zero. Jax remembered reading about it, but couldn't remember all the specifics of what qualified as functional zero. For some reason, it didn't mean there were zero homeless veterans on the streets.

Despite the state's recent efforts, for some like Leo, the trust had been lost a long time ago and it wasn't something he'd give back readily. Jax couldn't blame him. The government simply didn't take care of the men and women who had served for them the way they should. There was just no arguing the point. Leo wasn't going to go near the VA.

One of the doors opened and Leo and the familiar round face and balding head of Dr. Coleman stepped into the waiting area. Jax had met the doctor on previous visits with Leo.

Leo was stuffing a prescription bottle into one of his never-ending pockets as he nodded at something the doctor said to him.

Jax stood as the two approached. The doctor began to

turn toward the front reception desk, but Leo called out to him. "Hey, Doc, do I keep taking that other stuff, too?"

The doctor glanced around them and Jax had to stifle a laugh at the look of shock on the man's face. Leo had no sense of privacy or the need to keep his medical details to himself. The doctor's mind was probably shifting through all the HIPAA violations.

"No. These should replace your other medication." He nodded curtly and walked away.

"All set?" Jax asked as Leo patted his pockets, doing inventory.

"Yeah. Got some pills. Should feel better in a day or two, he says."

Jax didn't ask for details as they left the clinic, but he hoped the doctor was right.

* * *

Dr. Mark Coleman waited impatiently for the man to pick up. The nurse poked her head into his office and he had to swallow the urge to snap at her.

"Doctor, we've got Dena Miller in room three for you and there's an Allan Sykes here to drop something off. He says he needs to see you personally to have you sign for it."

"I need two minutes, Carol," he said turning his back on her as the phone continued to ring, unanswered. Sykes was the last person he wanted to see now.

"Yes, doctor," she said.

He heard the click of his office door shutting as the call connected.

"What do you want, doctor?" The voice was impatient and Coleman was struck again by the strength behind it. He never expected the older man to sound so young.

"I want out." Coleman lowered his voice even though his door was shut. He tugged at the collar of his shirt, undoing the top button. "Leo Kent was just here, presenting with the same symptoms as the others."

"Did you give him the increased dose?"

"Do you even care about what's going to happen to that man?" Coleman hissed into the phone, watching the door to his office. This was crazy. The researcher didn't seem to care about the obvious pattern that was forming. The man was insane.

"Of course I care. If I didn't think increasing the dosage would alleviate the risk, I wouldn't have you do it. I've tested this in the lab. The problem was caused by too little of the drug, not by the drug itself."

He injected just enough concern into his voice that most other people would buy it, but Coleman got the distinct feeling there wasn't a thread of truth behind it. He had no idea what the man's true purpose was, but he had begun to doubt everything he'd been told. He no longer believed they were working to save people at this point, and the thought made him sick.

Coleman didn't understand how this man could remain so calm when talking about the death of other human beings. He didn't have it in him to be that callous. "I'm done. I want—"

"I don't think you understand, Dr. Coleman. I don't care what you want. You no longer have a choice." All hint of concern—false or otherwise—was gone now. Nothing but coldness remained.

"What the hell is that supposed to mean?" He didn't need to ask the question. He knew exactly what it meant. The man had been playing him from the start. How he hadn't seen that earlier, he really didn't know.

"You and I both know what it means. You can't afford to walk away from this. I'll stop making payments and you'll be left trying to pay off your gambling debt without me. Do you really think that's wise? What do you think will happen to your family when you stop making payments?"

Coleman fell into his chair and let his head fall back. The people he owed money to would come after him, after his family. There was no doubt in his mind.

"I'll take that chance," he said, knowing he had to stop this. Maybe he could take his wife and daughter and go somewhere no one would find them. Start over. Only how did you start over when your livelihood depended on using your medical license? It's not like he could make a living without it, and if he used his license, they'd track him wherever he went.

There was one thing he'd figured out. The Genesio family didn't let you walk away from a debt. He looked down at his hand, where a nasty scar showed the evidence of what happened when you were late with payments.

"No, you won't," came the voice on the other end of the call. "Mr. Sykes should be there soon with another delivery. Now, just increase the dosage on anyone that comes through your door and send the data I'm paying you for."

He didn't wait for a response, and Coleman didn't offer one. He laid his phone down on his desk and closed his eyes.

What the hell have I done?

CHAPTER 6

LEO BLINKED as he looked into eyes he'd fallen in love with thirty-one years earlier. He'd fallen for her eyes first, and not long after, for the woman herself.

In thirty-one years, her eyes hadn't changed, and neither had his feelings for her. He'd once thought they would dull with time. No. That was wrong. He'd *hoped* they would dull with time.

"Lynn. I didn't expect ... I'm sorry, I uh—" Leo stepped back into his apartment, opening the door wider to let his wife—former wife—in. The instant he did it, he thought better of it, realizing how his place must look. Its size was only the first of the issues. He normally kept the place squared away and cleaned up, but with how his health had been, the sheets on the bed were a crumpled mess, and he had glasses and a dish with dried out toast lying on the side table.

Pride could be a nasty bitch. He'd lost his pride a long time ago, but somehow the thought of what Lynn must think of him still stabbed at him.

She entered and glanced around, looking as nervous to

be there as he felt to have her there. "Leo," was all she said and the voice took him back, washing him with emotions he couldn't name, much less handle.

He gestured to the couch, choosing to pretend the messy bed in the corner didn't exist. "I, uh, I guess Mia told you where I was."

"She did." Her eyes assessed him but he couldn't read her thoughts. The politeness in her tone just about slayed him. "Have you been here long?"

"In New Haven? Yeah. About, uh, ten years." He sat on the arm of the chair giving her the space her body language seemed to scream for. She perched on the edge of the couch looking for all the world like she might change her mind and bolt any second.

He could see her questions but she didn't press. He offered the information anyway. Getting sober had taught him there was no point in holding back or hiding things. It didn't get you anywhere but down.

"I spent a lot of years on the street, moving around the country. A little time in Florida, down in Texas. I came back this way ten years ago, but I wasn't sober until five years back." He looked her dead in the eye so she could see the truth in his words. "I haven't had a drop to drink in five years. Didn't get off the streets until a few months ago when a good friend helped me with this place." He glanced around again. "It's small, but it works for me."

She nodded and clutched at her bag in her lap.

"For what it's worth, Lynn, I am sorry." The words seemed limp as they dangled in the air between them. Worthless words that couldn't do a damned thing to erase the wrongs he'd done to her.

She raised her head at that and a look of sorrow marred the beautiful features of her face. She was still so stunningly gorgeous, she took his breath away. There was a strength to her he'd always been drawn to, and her eyes seemed to speak directly to his soul.

When the silence stretched he asked the question he'd been dreading. "Did you remarry?" A deep part of him wanted her to have found happiness, even if it wasn't with him, but an uglier part roared at the idea of her with another man. How stupid and selfish was that?

"Almost. It didn't work out." She paused before diving ahead. "For a long time, I tried to forgive you for what happened. I struggled with it, knowing I needed to let it go. To let you go."

God, he didn't want to hear, this, but he owed her that.

She shook her head at him, the corners of her lips lifting in a sad smile. "One day, I realized, I wasn't trying to forgive you for what happened that night. I was trying to forgive you for giving up. For leaving instead of fighting to find the man you were, to find the love we'd once had. To find *us* again."

He couldn't even hope to swallow the grapefruit in his throat as she spoke and he didn't know what to say in response. There wasn't anything to say, but he tried. "I couldn't take a chance on hurting you again." His voice cracked but he had to keep going. He wanted her to understand. "I couldn't risk that."

She took a deep breath and nodded. "I know. I know you did what you thought was right."

The silence stretched for a minute as she regarded him. He wanted with all his being to hide from her gaze, but he didn't. Lord knew he owed her that much. At least that much, and truth be told, a whole hell of a lot more.

"You need to tell Mia the truth."

"You never told her?" He couldn't hide the shock. He'd

always assumed Lynn would tell their daughter every horrible thing he'd done.

"It wasn't my place." Her eyes met his with a steely resolve he didn't feel in himself but respected the hell out of her for having. "I never wanted her to know that man before she had a chance to know who you really were. I told her about the man I know you to be. The soldier, the warrior, the good father."

He looked away but she continued.

"That night doesn't define you unless you let it, Leo. I think it's time for you to stop letting it."

She didn't wait for an answer, which was just as well because he didn't have one. He was speechless. He watched as she crossed the space and walked away.

* * *

Lynn pulled over a few blocks from the apartment building and tried to catch her breath. It didn't work. Instead, she had a good long cry in the confines of her car. Something she hadn't done in a long while. Her whole body shook. Seeing Leo had been more than she was able to handle.

It had brought back so much pain and heartache. A world of regret that stood between them like a concrete wall. It shocked her that after all these years, she would still give almost anything to have back the love they'd once shared. To rebuild what they'd felt for one another so long ago.

She dragged a tissue across her eyes and focused on steadying her breathing before she made the phone call she knew she needed to make.

A mother should always put her child's heart before her

own. And Mia had a chance now to know her father. Lynn would never begrudge her that.

"Mia?"

"Hey mom, what's up?"

"I saw your dad."

Only silence greeted her. She didn't blame Mia. Her daughter still held the anger of a young child when it came to her dad, and that made sense. That wound had been cut deep and early, and it was one that would stick with Mia no matter what her mother did to try to make it heal.

"I think you should see him again, sweetheart. I wouldn't tell you to do that if I thought he was still drinking or thought he would hurt you."

Silence. Her daughter was as stubborn as she was. She'd raised Mia to be strong, but she still sometimes silently cursed that strength when she had to run up against it herself.

"Mia, give him a chance to tell you what happened. He was a good man once, and I believe he still is. Let him tell you why he left."

"Why don't you tell me?"

She sighed. Mia had asked that question many times over the years, and she'd always simply given her the answer that it was complicated. The old speech of *it wasn't about you, it was about mommy and daddy*. "It's not my story to tell, Mia. It needs to come from your dad. But I would like you to give him the chance to tell you."

A quiet "all right" came after a pause, and Lynn hoped that could be the start of true healing for the heartbreak her daughter had carried all these years.

CHAPTER 7

"LO?" Jax was distracted as he picked up his phone. The spreadsheet on his computer was making his eyes cross. He didn't know how this company thought they could get funding from Sutton if they didn't get someone over there who understood how to organize numbers and run simple financial analysis. Unfortunately, their product had potential so it was worth it for him to see if he could wrap his head around what they were trying to convey with this shit.

"Is this Jaxon Cutter?"

Jax sat up and turned away from the computer. When a stranger sounded like that, there was only bad news to be had. His thoughts flew to his brothers first. All three of them were still overseas. But his parents would be the first to get news about them and it wouldn't be by phone.

"Yes."

"Mr. Cutter, I'm calling from New Haven Central Clinic. Leo Kent has you listed as his emergency contact."

Shit. Jax was up and out of his chair, grabbing his wallet and keys from his desk and headed toward the bank of elevators in the Sutton Capital lobby. "Has something happened?"

"Mr. Kent was transported to Yale New Haven Hospital by ambulance twenty minutes ago. He came in this morning to see the doctor and suffered a cardiac event while in the office."

"I don't understand." Jax stabbed repeatedly at the elevator button. Why the hell didn't the thing come? "Why didn't he call me? Who brought him there?"

She seemed a little taken aback and he couldn't really blame her. His questions made no sense and he couldn't really expect the poor woman to know why Leo hadn't called Jax for a ride. "I believe he took the bus, but I'm not sure."

He could hear voices in the background on her end of the line.

"I'm sorry, Mr. Cutter, you'll need to speak with the hospital now. As I said, he was transferred there. I can give you their information if you need it."

"No." He mashed the elevator button again. "Thank you, I'm on my way there."

Jax knew he wouldn't get information from anyone at the hospital over the phone. His best course would be to get down there in person right away. He texted the other members of his team to let them know he was leaving as the elevator descended at a snail's pace to the garage.

Not being able to do anything for Leo during the drive over was maddening. He wasn't a *do nothing* kind of guy. And it only got worse when he got to the ER.

"I understand, ma'am, but he listed me as his emergency contact at the clinic when he checked in there this morning. Can't you get that information from them?"

He looked at the nurse and hoped she'd take mercy on

him. She gave him the kind of look that told him she had too many other things to worry about right then.

"Please?" He hadn't been able to even confirm that Leo was there, much less what condition he was in.

"All right, I'll call over there." She gave him a look, but he let out a breath as he saw her walk behind the desk and pick up the phone.

Jax went back to searching the internet on his phone. He remembered that Mia worked at a law firm in Hartford from the letter he'd mailed for Leo. He was currently searching the terms *Mia, Kent, law,* and *Hartford* in hopes he'd hit on her firm.

Bingo. She was listed as the office manager at *Schuler and Koskoff.* Jax looked up and saw the nurse walking back to him before he had a chance to dial Mia's office.

He could see from the woman's face that she didn't have good news, but he didn't expect what she told him.

"The clinic confirmed you're Mr. Kent's emergency contact, Mr. Cutter. I'm afraid that doesn't mean that I have much news for you. Mr. Kent was admitted in full cardiac arrest. The doctors are working on him right now. I'll let you know as soon as I have an update on his condition."

He could see and hear the softness in her face and tone, and knew from that alone Leo wasn't in good shape. He once again began mentally hurling curses at himself. He'd known something was wrong with Leo. He should have gotten him to the clinic earlier. And when the doctor gave him more medicine, he should have insisted on more. Tests. Something.

"Thank you." He nodded and watched as she walked away, then lifted the phone to his ear knowing if he'd just gone to see Leo this morning, he might have gotten him help earlier.

"Mia Kent." Mia's voice was calm, cool, and collected, just the way, he had a feeling, she liked her world.

Jax hated that he was about to rock that sense of calm for her. Despite that their interactions had all been contentious, if he ever got to know Mia Kent, he was pretty sure he'd find he liked the woman. Well, liked her beyond just his first impression of gorgeous woman with soulful eyes and legs that didn't quit.

Holy hell. He cursed himself for thinking about Mia like that at a moment like this. What the hell was wrong with him?

"Hi, Mia. It's Jax Cutter. Your dad's friend. I'm calling from Yale New Haven Hospital." He rushed on, wanting to get this over with. "I'm sorry to call you at work, but I didn't know how else to get ahold of you and your mom."

"Yes?" There was a trepidation to her tone that kicked him in the gut.

"Your dad had a heart attack. I'm afraid I don't know much more than that. They're working on him now, but I thought you and your mom ..." Jax didn't really know what to say. *You and your mom, who apparently hadn't heard from your dad in years until I blew it and wrote a return address on an envelope, might want to come down here and see him?*

He didn't know what Mia and her mom would want to do or what Leo would want. All he knew was if his dad were sick—really, really sick like Leo seemed to be—he'd want to know about it. But Jax and his dad had a very different relationship than Mia and her dad did. Anyone with half a brain could piece that together.

"I just thought you should know," he finished lamely.

"Thank you."

Jax pulled the phone back from his ear and looked at it. Just as he'd thought. She'd hung up.

Well, he'd done what he could. It was up to Mia now to tell her mom and for the two of them to decide if they wanted to be here.

His cell phone buzzed as a text came through.

Let me know if you need anything.

Logan. Jax texted a quick reply updating Logan, knowing full well his friend would come down here if Jax so much as hinted he needed him. There wasn't anything Logan could do, though. All they could do was wait at this point.

CHAPTER 8

MIA WATCHED Jax from a distance as he paced the waiting room floor. Her mother stood by her side, but they had yet to enter the room. As they stood in the entranceway, she wondered if her mom was feeling the same odd detachment she was.

She felt numb. And a little angry. Okay, that wasn't true. She felt a lot angry. Jax was clearly worried sick about her dad. He seemed to glance at the front desk every few minutes as though hoping for an update that wasn't coming.

It made her angry that he had such a connection to her father. A father she'd needed, craved in her life all these years. A man who had left her and her mother alone all this time. Somehow Jax had built a relationship with that man and she'd never been given that chance.

"We have to go in sometime." Her mother's words were patient and soft.

Mia really wanted to turn to her and challenge the statement. *Did* they have to go in sometime? Not really. Her father hadn't been in her life in years. Why start now?

Instead, Mia nodded and stepped forward, triggering

the double doors to slide open with an electronic *whoosh*. The air conditioning hit full blast and Jax's gaze found hers instantly, deep brown eyes softening as he came across the room to them.

"I haven't heard anything yet," he said, speaking directly to her, but turning to her mother right away. "I'm Jax Cutter. I would have called you directly, but I didn't know how to reach you."

His politeness was the kind bred into a person from birth and Mia had the odd feeling he had been raised by a family where politeness and manners was not only expected but demanded. Kindness, too, she thought, then shook her head. She didn't know why her brain refused to function at the moment. Maybe it was a coping mechanism. Focus on the gorgeous military man in front of you so you don't have to face the reality of your situation.

She didn't know how she knew he had been in the military. She hadn't even noticed the prosthetic leg the first time she met him, but she'd seen it the second. That could be from an accident or any number of other things, though.

Maybe it was the way his hair still had that *high and tight* kind of look to it, or whatever they called it. Or she'd simply assumed it since he was friends with her dad.

The runaway train to bizarro land that her head seemed to be on was cut off by the approach of a man in scrubs.

The man glanced from her mother, to Mia, and back to Jax before speaking.

"Jax Cutter?"

"That's me." Jax seemed to notice the way the doctor took in both women. "This is Leo's daughter and—" he stopped and looked to Mia's mom as though realizing they hadn't been introduced.

"I'm Lynn Kent, Leo's wife."

Mia noticed her mom didn't say ex-wife and wondered at that. She had, in fact, divorced Mia's father several years after he'd taken off. She still used his last name, of course, and Mia wasn't stupid. She knew her mom had never stopped loving him. Maybe in her eyes she still saw herself as Leo's wife.

The doctor nodded and that's when Mia knew. There was a tightness to his mouth and grim determination he couldn't hide. Her father was dead. She didn't need to be told.

She turned and took a couple of steps away even as the doctor spoke.

"I'm sorry, but we weren't able to save him. Mr. Kent suffered a catastrophic cardiac event. I understand he was under the care of a physician for his heart?"

Mia heard Jax's voice respond, but couldn't make out his words. She felt like the ocean was roaring in her ears. She turned and walked back to the group, thinking this probably wasn't something she should be missing, and almost wanting to laugh at the strange out-of-body feeling she had and the way her mind seemed to be functioning in slow motion.

She tuned out much of what they were saying as the doctor talked about the measures they'd taken to revive him. She didn't miss the distress in Jax's voice as he asked if earlier treatment could have saved him or why the doctor at the clinic hadn't been able to see this coming the other day when Jax had taken him in.

The doctor didn't seem to have many answers, explaining instead that oftentimes there was no warning and nothing that could have been done to save him. The look on Jax's face told Mia he didn't believe the man, that he'd be doing a lot of blaming aimed at himself over this.

The doctor gestured to the nurse hovering behind him. "Margaret will help you with the paperwork and get his effects for you. We'll release the body to the funeral home of your choice once the proper paperwork has been completed."

Her mother turned toward Jax. "He wanted to be cremated."

Jax nodded.

"I'll go see about the paperwork," her mother said as the doctor walked away, and the nurse stepped into his place, leading her mom down the hall.

Jax stepped close to Mia, taking her hand and squeezing it. She looked up at him, startled at the contact.

"I'm sorry, Mia. I know you just found him."

She lifted a shoulder and let it drop. "It's not like I knew him."

Warm eyes assessed her. "Why do you do that?"

"Do what?" She looked away, glancing to where her mom was talking to the nurse. Cremation, her mother had said. She guessed it made sense they would have talked about what they wanted when they were married. Her father had been away at war. There'd always been a very real possibility of his not coming home and her mother needing to plan a funeral.

"Pretend it doesn't matter."

She looked back to the man in front of her and schooled her features. She wasn't having this conversation with a stranger, and most definitely not with *this* stranger.

"Because it doesn't." Mia turned and walked away. She'd wait for her mom in the parking lot, away from eyes that saw more than she wanted them to see.

* * *

Jax stood on one side of the emergency room gurney, while Lynn stood on the other side. She looked at Leo with such longing, such powerful love still evident in her eyes, and Jax was surprised to realize she still loved Leo.

Mia hadn't come in to say goodbye to her father. Jax wondered if she would grow to regret that someday.

"I'm sorry, Lynn. If I'd known he was this sick ..." Jax cut off as his voice broke. He felt like just minutes before he'd been sitting at his desk when the phone rang. How did this happen?

The laughter and life had left his friend's face. They'd removed the breathing tube and IVs, but the evidence of the needles going into his arms was clear, and the devices stood nearby on a tray. There was a hopelessness to the discarded tools, as if they underscored the finality of what had happened.

Jax was no stranger to death. He'd seen death often and violently, but this still rocked him. Somehow a death unexpected was worse than even what he'd witnessed in conflict.

"Oh, honey," she said, and Jax recognized the mother in her. It seemed all mothers knew how to comfort this way. "There wasn't anything you could have done."

He looked away. He didn't know that, but he appreciated her trying to make him feel better.

Lynn was looking back at Leo now. "I had hoped—"

She didn't finish the thought and Jax wondered if her hopes had been for her and Leo or Leo and Mia. Maybe both.

CHAPTER 9

"YOU'LL NEED to get more medication to Coleman." The man didn't bother to look through the data Sykes had handed him.

He carefully slipped the papers Coleman had sent him out of the envelope. He glanced at the data and set the envelope aside. He had more use for the envelope than the data.

"No problem." Sykes nodded, standing in that hovering way he had, as if waiting to jump into action at any moment. If Sykes thought anything of the fact that he wore gloves, he didn't question it.

At the start of their association, the man had thought Sykes was a yes man. It was why he'd chosen him. His connection to Simms Pharmaceutical had also helped, of course.

Now, he knew better. Coleman had called again. He was getting pressure from the police, from one of the homeless man's friends. And Coleman was the type of man to crack under that pressure. He couldn't have that. He'd have to address the situation before it went too far.

Sykes didn't question the man the way Coleman did, and there were two reasons for that. The first was arrogance, a trait that often slayed men. It had once ruled him, in fact. The second was greed. They combined to make Sykes the perfect man for the job. He was too confident to think the man would never need him—to realize he was replaceable and expendable—and he was greedy enough to overlook a lot of things that might give another man pause.

"Triple the quantity for the next delivery and bring these instructions to the doctor."

He printed off the directions and handed them over to Sykes.

Sykes looked at the sheet then frowned. "You sure about these numbers? That's a big increase. I'm not sure I can produce it quickly enough to keep up this schedule."

He looked at Sykes and raised his brows.

Sykes shrugged. "I'm just saying, I'll need more money to make this happen. I'll have to be producing around the clock unless you bring in someone else. If it's just me getting the job done," he lifted his chin, "I'm going to need more."

He watched him long enough for Sykes to begin to squirm. He didn't care about paying him more money. He just wanted Sykes to know he couldn't make a habit of this.

He nodded. "Fine. Now get it done and get the meds to Coleman. I don't have time to screw around."

* * *

The memorial service was quiet and small. There were people from Jax's office who'd come to support him, but the largest group of people were the fifteen or twenty men and women who'd known her father when they lived on the streets with him. They didn't speak with anyone other than Jax, but their desire to pay their respects to the man she barely knew was clear.

She saw Jax speak quietly to each of them. They seemed to know him, and she wondered if he had helped a lot of them out, or if he'd simply known them through her dad. She still hadn't found out how he knew her dad, and it occurred to her now that maybe he worked with a lot of homeless people in New Haven. Maybe he volunteered at the shelter or something along those lines. For all she knew, he might work there. She simply had no idea.

Mia sat next to her mom and beat back tears as the minister spoke of her father's military record. She hadn't known he'd received the Navy Cross or that he'd gone to Iraq in the Gulf War, not once but twice, before coming home with an injury that ended his military career and, she suspected, tore their family apart.

Her father's remains had been cremated and would be sent to the National Cemetery in Houston for interment. Jax had arranged that. Apparently any military service man or woman can request their ashes be interred in a national cemetery. It would be nice, she thought, for him to be honored in that way.

Jax stood and moved to the front of the church when the minister invited him, standing behind the podium in his dress uniform. She had been surprised to see him in the white dress uniform of a Sailor, although she didn't know why that should surprise her.

Her father had been in the Marines, so she tended to picture military uniforms as the navy and red of the Marines, which really made very little sense.

Mia took her mother's hand and squeezed it as her mom

wiped at her nose with a tissue. She couldn't begin to imagine what her mother was feeling.

It struck Mia again that she hadn't asked Nick to come to the funeral with her. And he hadn't offered. She didn't know why she hadn't asked. She just hadn't felt like sharing this part of her with him, but now she wished for his presence by her side. For the calm way he'd hold her hand and simply be there for her.

Jax cleared his throat. "I'm afraid I'm not very good at this. I'd like to do justice to the man we're paying our respects to today, but I know I can't." He looked to the group of homeless men and women and seemed to speak to them for a moment. "It doesn't seem fair, does it?"

He laughed a bit, but there was a bitterness to it. He didn't have to voice what he was thinking. Mia knew everyone in the room was thinking the same thing. *Leo had just gotten off the streets. Why now?*

Jax swallowed hard and began again. "Leo and I never talked about his Navy Cross. I honestly don't even remember how I knew he had it." Jax took a piece of paper from his coat pocket and unfolded it. "I looked up the details of the citation."

His eyes scanned the small group. "Only two Navy Cross Awards were awarded during all of the Gulf War. One of those was awarded to Captain Leo Eddie Kent, United States Marine Corps."

He looked down at the paper and read the citation aloud. The language was formal and filled with military designations and terms she didn't understand. The story behind the award was clear, though, even to Mia's untrained ears. Under heavy enemy fire, her father led his Company in repeated attacks on the enemy, taking out forty-two enemy Armored Personnel Carriers. The Citation spoke of her father as having decisive leadership, unlimited courage in the face of danger, and utmost devotion to duty. It spoke of the lengths he went to in bringing all but three of his men out of there alive.

Mia pressed her hand over her mouth as emotions swamped her. What would have made an American Hero leave her mother and her behind? What could have made him walk away from them? Abandon them when he clearly showed such loyalty and duty to those around him overseas?

Jax put the paper away and looked around the room again.

"I only met Leo a couple of years ago, but I met him at a time when I greatly needed someone to reach out and pull me off a ledge." His eyes turned back to the other side of the church now, and Mia felt as though he were speaking only to her.

"When I came home from Iraq, I was thankful to be alive. Thankful to be mostly in one piece." A laugh trickled through the room and Jax smiled a wry smile before continuing. "But despite all that, I had a little trouble figuring out who I could be if I wasn't FMF Corpsman Cutter. If I wasn't *Doc*. That's who I was. It was all I was. All I'd wanted to be since I was a little boy."

He looked around the room and Mia had a feeling it wasn't easy for him to admit any weakness to anyone.

"My brothers are still in the military. My father is a career Navy man. My mother is a military wife, a military mom. I didn't know where I fit any more. Didn't have a purpose, a plan. I was flailing."

He paused as he looked at the urn holding Leo's ashes and the photo of her father in his military uniform as a young man. Her mother had provided the picture.

"Leo and I started hanging out and one day, he looked at

me. I never really did figure out how he knew what was eating at me. I hadn't told him. He just looked at me and said, *one step at a time. One foot in front of the other.* It was a mantra I knew well. There were times I was out there in the desert telling myself that same thing. Just keep moving. Just keep going. Do one thing, then the next. The shit would hit the fan and all hell would rain down on us, and I'd think, keep moving. I'd go from one injury to the next, only allowing myself to be in *that* moment with *that* Marine.

Leo got that. He said, *triage your shit. Move on. One day, you won't feel so damned out of place. You won't feel like you're half-assed kilter in a straight and narrow world.*" Jax glanced at the minister and apologized before turning to the mourners again. "He was right. I did what he said, and one day I realized, I was all right. Things were okay and I was going to find a place in the world without the military."

Mia watched as Jax shook his head and let out a bark of laughter. "Leo was with me through all of that. He asked me once why I was helping him. Why I wanted to hang around with a useless old man like him."

Jax's eyes cut back to Mia again and her heart stilled as she waited.

"He was a good man who helped me more than he'll ever know. I'd imagine he was like that for a lot of the people he met on this walk in life we all have to make. He'd struggled for so long himself, but five years ago, he managed to leave alcohol behind. He left it behind and began to reach out to those he met, helping them. By the time I met him, he was a different man. He was a man who helped those around him. I think he touched a lot of us in his own quiet way despite the demons he was battling himself."

He turned to Leo's image and saluted, the quiet around him thick with emotion. Mia saw a few of the men in the group stand and salute as well and she wondered about their service. She wondered if they were fighting demons.

"Goodbye, my friend."

As Jax walked back to the pew, he held Mia's gaze and she found herself unable to look away.

CHAPTER 10

"ARE you sure I can't take you to lunch?" Jax looked between mother and daughter, feeling awful that there wasn't more he could say or do. He couldn't imagine what it would be like to finally find someone you'd been missing all this time and then lose them so quickly.

"Thank you, but it's not necessary." Lynn Kent had a gentle quiet way about her, but there was strength there, too.

She had insisted on driving Jax back to his house after he, Mia, and Lynn had all stayed after the rest of the mourners had left the funeral home.

Jax nodded and handed his card through Mia's open window. "Call me if you need anything. Either of you."

"Thank you, Jax," Lynn said, but Mia only gave him a small smile. She'd been quiet the whole ride back to his house. He knew they planned to stay the night in a hotel and drive back to Hartford in the morning, and for all the world, he wanted to extend the time he had with Mia. He wanted to comfort her in some way.

Not in *some* way. He wanted to reach out and pull her

to him. He wanted to wrap her up and hold her and make this better for her.

Which was stupid really. He barely knew her.

As he stood and waved while the car pulled away, he wondered if it was simply his way of trying to extend his time with Leo. Of somehow not saying goodbye to a man who'd been his closest friend and confidant for the last few years.

He turned and looked up at the front door of his house. It was always empty and quiet when he came home to it, but today the effect seemed intensified.

Jax turned away from the walkway and toward the driveway, pulling the keys to his Jeep out of his pocket. He'd told Lynn and Mia he would clean out Leo's apartment and take care of getting anything either of them might want to keep. He'd never been one to delay something that had to be done, no matter how unpleasant the task. Now was as good a time as any.

As he pulled up to the apartment building that had been Leo's home for only a few short months, the irony hit him once again. Leo had been off the streets for the first time in years. He'd had shelter and regular food. He'd had a place to sleep that was safe and protected him from the cold or the heat. How was it that his life had been taken now of all times?

The plastic bag from the hospital containing Leo's belongings sat on the passenger seat of his car as it had for the past three days. He grabbed it and walked up the three flights of steps to Leo's place. He'd get things cleaned out and then see what kind of cleaning supplies Leo kept on hand. He'd give the place a once over before turning the keys over to the super.

Jax stilled as he approached the apartment door, seeing

the door slightly ajar. The lock bore the marks of the effort it had taken for someone to break in, scratches evident in the metal surrounding the lock.

He slowly pushed open the door, standing to the side as he scanned the room. He could see all but the bathroom in the little space. Empty. And other than the bedside table drawers being open, it looked mostly undisturbed. The small television stood on its stand in the corner, just as it always had.

Jax crossed to the bathroom door and peered in. No one in there, but the medicine cabinet stood open. Band-Aids and mouthwash were all that graced the shelves.

He cursed as he walked back over to the apartment door and nudged it shut with his foot before pulling out his phone.

"Hey Chad," he said when his friend picked up the phone. Chad Thompson had been one of the people from Sutton Capital to attend Leo's funeral out of respect for Jax, and Jax appreciated the gesture. Chad was also former military, so he understood more than others that the bond between veterans was strong. He'd never questioned why Jax had helped get Leo off the streets. "You have a friend on the New Haven Police Force, right?"

"Yeah, Jarrod Harmon. A detective. Everything all right?"

"Uh, maybe." Jax looked around at the room and felt a little foolish. He probably shouldn't be calling this in at all. There didn't seem to be anything missing. "You know what? It's nothing. I shouldn't have called."

"*What's* nothing?" Chad pressed.

"I came to clean out Leo's apartment and it's been broken into. The lock was picked and there are a few things out of place. The weird thing is, nothing seems to be missing." As he spoke, he crossed the room and picked up the plastic bag from the hospital that he'd set on the couch on his way in. "Except ..."

He tore the plastic and pulled out Leo's things, checking through the vest pockets.

"Except, what?"

"His meds are gone." The two medicine bottles Leo had had at the clinic just days earlier were gone. Jax walked around the apartment, looking on the little dinette table, the small piece of kitchen counter that flanked the sink, then back into the bathroom for another look. "He had medicine he was taking. I saw it the other day when we were at the clinic but it's not here and it's not in his jacket pockets."

"Maybe they kept it at the hospital?" Chad sounded like he didn't know any better than Jax did whether that would be protocol or not.

Jax frowned and looked around again. "Why would someone break in and then not take anything? There's a TV here. It's small but it's actually pretty new and easy enough to carry off." He was talking to himself now more than Chad.

"Let me call Jarrod and see what he thinks. See if it's worth filling out a report or anything." Chad paused. "Shit, I'm sorry. I didn't mean that the way it sounded."

"I get it." Jax said. He did. Leo was gone. "You'll let me know what he says?"

"Yeah. Hang tight. I'll call you back in a few."

Jax stood in the center of the apartment and waited, not knowing if he should touch anything else.

Chad texted back quickly to say Jax should wait. Jarrod was on his way.

He doubted very many people calling about a break in where virtually nothing was missing had two detectives show up on scene, but there was Chad's friend with another man fifteen minutes later.

"Jarrod Harmon," the tall man said as he put his hand out for Jax to shake. Jarrod Harmon had the firm handshake and experienced gaze of a veteran detective, and he had an air of calm confidence that set some cops apart from others. His partner was shorter, but looked no less capable for it.

Jarrod gestured to the man by his side who'd been silent so far. "This is my partner Cal Mullen." Mullen nodded. He was shorter and bulkier than Jarrod with hair that was cut in the standard high and tight cut of a cop. Jax had a feeling people likely wrote him off as a meathead since he looked like he spent hours in a gym each day, but there was a sharp intelligence to his eyes.

"Jax Cutter. Yeah, Leo was a good man. Marines." He glanced away, not really wanting to talk about Leo. "I hope I didn't get you guys down here for nothing. I don't think there's anything missing other than Leo's prescription meds."

Jarrod shrugged. "Doesn't hurt to have a report on file." He walked around the apartment, pausing to look through the stack of mail on the kitchen table. "Bills are still here. That's good."

Cal explained. "Sometimes people are hoping to get personal information they can use to get a credit card or use someone's identity. It's possible someone in the building heard about your friend's death and came looking for that, but this mail looks undisturbed."

Jax had to agree. The small stack of envelopes stood tucked between the bottle of hot sauce Leo kept on the table and the wall the table stood against.

"The night stand's drawers were open when I came in and the medicine cabinet was open. I can't find his pill bottles. Other than that, I can't come up with anything else that could be missing."

Jarrod looked around the kitchen counter before coming over to where Jax and Cal waited. "Did your friend keep any cash here or any medals? Pictures or honors from when he served?"

"Shit." Jax crossed to the twin bed and knelt down to pull the bedspread aside. "I can't believe I forgot to look."

He slid a small box out from under the bed and opened it. He'd seen Leo tuck it under the bed when they'd moved him into the apartment, but he'd never asked what was in it. He had a feeling it held the few valuables Leo treasured and held onto all those years he was on the street.

There was the wad of folded twenty-dollar bills Jax had snuck back into Leo's vest pocket the week before. Jax put that aside and pulled out the Navy Cross Leo had been awarded, handling it with a sense of reverent awe. Underneath were pictures. Pictures of Lynn Kent and a smiling little girl he recognized immediately as Mia.

He stood and tilted the box in Jarrod's direction letting him see that the contents, including the cash, were still there.

Jarrod and Cal wore nearly identical frowns as Jarrod spoke. "Do you happen to know what the prescription medications were?"

Jax shook his head. "No. I tried not to pry about things like that. I took him to the clinic because he wasn't feeling well. I know he got some meds from the doc that day. He didn't say what they were. I didn't press it. He did ask the doc about something he'd given him before. Actually, the doctor seemed to get a little weird when Leo asked about that."

Now it was Jax's turn to frown. He hadn't thought

much of it at the time but looking back, the doctor's discomfort seemed somewhat odd.

"How so?" Jarrod prompted him.

"The doctor walked out with him to the waiting room and Leo asked if he should still take the other stuff the doctor had given him. It seemed to make him really uncomfortable. I assumed it was just a HIPPA thing, you know? The doctor not wanting to talk about Leo's personal medical info in front of anyone else." Jax shrugged. That probably was all that had been going through the doctor's head. He was making something over nothing.

"Do you know his doctor's name?" Cal asked.

"Yeah. Dr. Coleman. At least, that's who he saw the last couple of times I brought him in. I think he's seen one or two of the other doctors, too. It's a walk-in clinic so it depends a bit on who's in that day."

A knock came from the open apartment door and a uniformed officer stuck his head in. "Detective Harmon?"

"Hey Manny, come on in. Jax, this is Patrolman Vasquez. He's going to fill out the police report for you. Manny, this is Jax Cutter. He discovered the break in. The apartment tenant is recently deceased. So far, it appears all that's missing are some prescription meds."

The young officer nodded, and pulled a notepad and pen from his chest pocket, old school style, and started jotting notes.

Jax hesitated, and looked around. "I feel like maybe I'm making something out of nothing." As he said it, the buzzing at the back of his neck that had kept him alive in so many situations overseas kicked in. It was that buzzing that had meant the difference between life and death for him on a number of occasions. On the other hand, when that IED had hit, he hadn't had a clue he was about to step on it.

"Except you don't." Jarrod's voice didn't contain judgment. Cal was silent again, but Jax didn't get the sense the man was judging him at all for calling them down here.

"Sorry. It's just something in my gut telling me there's something wrong." Jax looked at the detectives and hoped they got what he was saying.

"I understand gut," Jarrod said. "Listen, I can't promise you I can throw a ton of resources at this or anything. I'm not going to flat out lie to you. But we will stop by and talk to the doc and we'll have the report on file for the break in if we need it."

"Thank you," Jax said, grateful the guys hadn't laughed in his face.

CHAPTER 11

THE KNOCK on the door was quiet enough that it might not wake anyone else, but Jax had been a light sleeper even before the military. Now, he could be awake and be on his feet in seconds at the slightest of sounds. It also helped that he'd fallen asleep in front of the TV in the den right off his front hall.

He didn't expect to see Mia Kent on his doorstep at one in the morning. He sure as hell didn't expect her to look like she did. He could only describe her as rumpled, but on her it was somehow sexy. Like her uptight, buttoned-up look had been pulled apart and she had that sexy librarian vibe going that all men fantasize about.

Well, at least, he did. He didn't know about all men, but Mia had just walked out of one of his dreams with her hair pulled out of its ponytail, and her shoes dangling from two fingers. His body tightened just looking at her.

Christ. He brushed a hand down his face. He could *not* be having those thoughts about *this* woman. It didn't matter that she wasn't raised by Leo. She was Leo's daughter, none-theless.

He looked outside but saw no car, which was probably a good thing. He could smell something sweet on her, but the underlying scent was alcohol.

"How did you get here?"

"I walked," she said, handing him her shoes and walking into his home. Her arm brushed across his chest as she walked by. She smelled like coconuts and he wondered if it was her shampoo or the drinks she'd clearly had. He wanted to pull her close and tangle his hands through her hair. Wanted to bury his face in it and see if that was where the light sweet scent was coming from. He wanted to know if she tasted like coconuts, too.

Christ, he was screwed.

Jax eyed her as he shut the door and leaned his back against it. This visit had bad news written all over it. The woman was his dead best friend's daughter. She was drinking. And she'd just found, and then lost, the father she hadn't had a chance to know.

Top it off with the fact that he was thinking all kinds of crap he shouldn't be thinking about her, and the whole thing was a disaster in the making.

He wondered if he should tell her about the break-in at Leo's place, then thought better of it. He'd tell her tomorrow. He took the two steps over to his side table where he kept his car keys and grabbed them and his wallet.

"Come on. I'll drive you back to the hotel."

Mia spun toward him, opening her mouth, but tipped to the side before she could say a word. "Whoa!"

Jax reached out and steadied her, taking a step closer to her as she gripped his forearms. *Yeah. This is bad.*

"I don't want to go back to the hotel." She looked up at him with those big brown eyes and they weren't closed off to him like they usually were. There was an open vulnerability to her tonight. She was hurting.

Jax stepped backward, clamping his hands onto Mia's arms and holding her away from him. Mostly to keep himself from doing something he'd regret. She was enticing as all hell, but she was also drunk. Her eyes were glassy with the effects of it, and if her daytime reaction to him was any indication, this wasn't something she would want if she were able to think straight.

Leo's daughter. Leo's daughter. Leo's daughter.

He kept the chant going in his head as he stepped backward, letting his hands fall to his sides.

"My boyfriend didn't come to the funeral," she said.

He took another step back.

He didn't know why the news of a boyfriend was such a slap in the face. In fact, it was exactly what they needed. A big, giant wall between them. A wall with barbed wire and maybe some cut glass on top so he wouldn't scale the fucker.

"I'm sorry," she said, surprise on her face. "That made it sound like I was ... like I wanted ... Oh my gosh." She put her hands over her mouth as if she could stop the verbal hemorrhaging she had going on and Jax laughed, breaking some of the tension that clouded the small room.

"Come sit down," he said. "We can talk, okay?" He understood that she might be reeling. He'd felt like he was floating along in some nightmare he couldn't wake up from all day. He hadn't realized how much he'd come to rely on Leo to keep him feeling grounded lately.

She watched him for a minute with the guarded gaze he was used to seeing in her, then sat on the couch, drawing her feet up under her. It struck him that she treated him like women had treated him before he lost his leg. She treated him like any other man.

He'd had some women who seemed to be unusually drawn to him *because* of his leg. Others had babied him. He'd been talking to a woman in a bar on one of the rare occasions he'd gone out with people at work. Minutes into talking to her, she'd looked stricken.

"I should offer you my seat," she said, sliding off the stool she'd been sitting on. He hadn't stuck around. What man wants a woman to offer him her seat?

Mia never acted like he was different from anyone else. He shook off the thought and sat on the other end of the couch, then pushed the water bottle he'd been drinking before he passed out her way.

"Hydrate. You'll regret this less in the morning."

She lifted the bottle to her lips and sipped. "I don't drink alcohol very often." She said, a crinkle in her brows as she tried to focus on him.

It was only now he realized just how drunk she was. Her speech was slurred and her eyes were starting to close. She was lucky no one had picked her up on the mile walk from downtown to his place. Anything could have happened to her out there, especially in this condition.

"I can see that." He grinned and she laughed back. It wasn't one of those annoying school girl giggles. It was genuine.

Her smile went away, though, and she leaned her head on her arm. "What was he like?" Her question was quiet, as though she wasn't sure she wanted to know the answer.

Jax blew out a breath. He didn't know what to say. Her dad was a different man to him than he was to Mia. In Mia's mind, Leo was the villain who left her when she needed him.

Knowing Leo had walked away from his wife and child had been hard for Jax to stomach. He'd felt no small amount of anger toward his friend when he heard that. It had occurred to Jax that his friends Jack and Kelly had a daughter just about the age Mia had been when Leo left her. Their daughter was happy and laughing, so trusting in her parents at that age. The confusion Mia must have felt as a little girl when her father simply vanished must have been awful.

He couldn't imagine leaving his wife and child. Couldn't imagine what brought a man to that point. Even with all the shit he'd seen overseas. But every war was different, every soldier his own man. How Leo coped with what he saw and did was different than how Jax had coped.

"He was a good man." Jax sat up a little trying to put into words what he was feeling and thinking. "I met Leo after he'd been clean and sober for years. He didn't tell me about you, but he did talk about regrets. Regrets a person couldn't get past. I think he was talking about you and your mom."

He could see her struggling with something and knew she probably had a million questions about her dad. Sadly, they were questions he didn't have answers to.

Despite that, he tried to offer her something. "I meant what I said at the funeral. His being there for me really helped pull me through. I don't know why he couldn't do the same for himself years before. Why he drank so much. What he was running from all this time."

"Me neither," she said, and he saw tears slip down her cheeks.

He moved closer and wiped at the tears, her sadness cutting through him. "Have you asked your mom what happened?"

"She said it was his story to tell me. Of course, that was before he died."

"Will you ask her again now?"

"I don't know. I don't know if I'm ready to hear it, to be honest. Something tells me there's a lot more to it than you or I could imagine."

"Why do you say that?" he asked.

"It's just this sense I've always had. My mom would never talk about that with me when I was little. She would tell me what a good man he was, that he'd fought for his country. That he had to leave. But there was always something more there that she wasn't saying. Like it was almost this big live thing. Like a secret that had a life of its own."

He nodded.

"Can I tell you something horrible?" she whispered and he didn't know if he should say yes or no. When she was sober, would she want him to know whatever it was she was about to divulge?

She didn't wait for an answer, though. "Sometimes, I wish he'd had a great life. That I'd discovered he was living the good life, with plenty of money and a home and job. Maybe even a wife and children—a new family."

Jax waited for her to explain what she meant.

She pulled her legs up and wrapped her arms around her knees, chin resting on them as she stared at the wall, eyes not appearing to see the room around her. "It would have been easy to hate him then. Easy to just walk away and not care about him."

They sat quietly for a while longer before Jax saw more than a couple of yawns coming from her. Her eyes kept closing. She'd open them with a start and manage to keep them open for a minute or two before they closed again.

"Come on," he stood and put a hand out, pulling her from the couch. "You take my bed. I was sleeping on the couch anyway when you got here."

She tried a token protest but the argument didn't last long. As Jax turned out the light to his room and shut the door, he noticed how small Mia looked, curled on her side in his bed. Small and hurting and needing answers. She might not want to know what demons chased her dad away all those years ago, but Jax had a feeling it was a story she needed to hear.

CHAPTER 12

IT TOOK Mia a few minutes to realize where she was. The pounding headache and whirling in her stomach didn't help any. The confusion was probably multiplied by the fact that she expected to sleep in a hotel room the night before, so it wasn't like she planned to wake in her own bed.

When she didn't wake in either her bed or the hotel, it took a few minutes for her location to sink in.

Ugh. Jax's house.

She couldn't for the life of her remember why she'd thought it was a good idea to walk to his house.

Oh yeah. Nick.

She'd called Nick after the funeral. Talking to him hadn't helped. She had no idea why. He'd said all the right things. He hadn't said anything about her dad being a deadbeat or how she shouldn't have let him back into her life. He'd been there for her despite the fact she knew he hadn't agreed with her decision to go meet her dad.

But talking to Nick hadn't helped her. She'd wanted to talk to Jax.

She sat up, then had to lean back against the headboard,

trying to block out the sun with one hand. Her stomach bottomed out, followed by a little swirl to double up on the yuck factor she was feeling. She closed her eyes and waited a few minutes for the feeling to pass before opening them again.

Mia looked around on the floor but didn't see her shoes. She still wore the black slacks and grey blouse she'd worn to her father's memorial service, and later to the bar. Her jacket was nowhere to be found, so it must be with her shoes. She got herself up slowly and visited the bathroom in the master bedroom.

She expected more bare bones décor in the master bedroom and bathroom. Maybe because Jax was a guy, or maybe because of his military background. But his bedroom actually felt like someone had put some thought into decorating it. The walls were gray with white trim, and his sheets and comforter coordinated with the theme. He had an acoustic guitar in the corner and a basketball and one sneaker on the floor by the closet. The bathroom was a deep plum color, with gray towels and an abstract painting on the wall that featured complementary colors.

Tired bloodshot eyes met her in the mirror and her face was marked by the wrinkles of the sheet she'd had tucked under her cheek as she'd slept. *Great.* She ran her fingers through her hair, trying to straighten the tangles a bit, then rinsed her mouth with water. She felt like she'd eaten a truckload of sawdust instead of the five or six Mai Tais she'd downed. She'd gone with them because fruity had seemed like a good idea. And who would have thought you could get so drunk on such a fruity concoction?

She went back into the bedroom and found her cell phone on the nightstand.

Where are you? Call me! I'm worried!

Wow. She should win daughter of the year. She'd pretty much forgotten that she and her mom were sharing a hotel room. Her poor mother had texted several times in the last hour.

I'm sorry mom! I'm fine. Be back in a few. She wondered if she could claim she'd gone out for an early morning walk, then looked down at her attire. Not likely. Her mother was no idiot.

Mia turned the knob to the bedroom door as quietly as she could. She held her cellphone in one hand as she tiptoed through the house. She'd need to find her shoes and get out before Jax woke up.

"Boo."

Mia jumped forward and damned near out of her skin at the quiet voice behind her. *Close* behind her. How the hell had he snuck up on her without a sound?

She turned to glare at the man in question as she put a hand to her chest.

Wow. The man in question was drawing a tee-shirt over his own chest—his naked chest. Mia stared as he drew the fabric down. The cut torso and tanned skin was mouth-watering, to say the least. She'd caught a glimpse of the tribal tattoo that covered his left shoulder and came down his bicep.

Her gaze followed the tattoo up his neck, eventually resting back on his face, where he gave her one of those grins that said he'd caught her looking. She raised her eyebrows. Of course she'd looked. What did he think she was going to do?

"Want some breakfast?" He walked past her in the hallway and headed right toward what she guessed would be the kitchen.

"Um, no that's all right. I'll just head out." She slowed

as she walked through the den, looking around for her shoes. She vaguely recognized the room from the night before. Her shoes sat by the couch, her jacket was folded over the back of a chair.

Jax poked his head back out of the kitchen and gave her a look she imagined he'd used in the military. "Get your skinny ass in here and have a proper breakfast."

He didn't wait for an answer.

Skinny ass?

Mia left her stuff where it was and padded into the kitchen, finding him digging through the refrigerator. She had a perfect view of his backside, and it wasn't going to be easy to turn away from that. The man looked like he was still in the military. All tight muscles and chiseled edges under the cargo shorts and tee.

She burst out laughing when her eyes wandered down to his legs. The left leg was the prosthesis she'd seen him wear most often. The top two thirds of it was glossy black with a subtle snake skin pattern. The bottom was matte black and looked like it was made of some sort of hard plastic that bent forward to make a kind of landing device for him to step on. What made her laugh was the tattoo on the other leg. *Poser.*

Jax turned and grinned. "That's how your dad and I met. He spotted the tattoo and cracked up. We got to talking." He shrugged like it was nothing, but to Mia each word was gold. Despite the warring emotions she felt whenever she thought of her dad, she wanted to know more about Leo.

"So, what, then you guys just started hanging out and you set him up in an apartment?" She hadn't meant it to sound the way it did. Like an accusation of some kind. It had just struck her as odd for some time that he'd paid for her dad's place.

He looked up from where he was scrambling eggs. "Yeah. That's about the gist of it." It was his turn to shrug.

She tilted her head and waited, but he didn't say any more. He busied himself with popping a few pieces of bread into the toaster and moving the eggs around in the pan as they cooked before continuing.

"The thing is, you just don't leave a man behind, you know?"

He looked up at her but she shook her head just a little. She didn't know. She couldn't really understand the military experience. She would have been a military brat if her dad had stayed. But as it was, she and her mom had left that life when he'd taken off. It wasn't the first time she'd wondered how different her life would have been if her dad hadn't left. Not necessarily better. Not necessarily worse. Simply different.

Jax seemed to struggle for words for a minute. "When you're over there and your world can fall apart in a heartbeat, and you're seeing things, hearing things—hell, smelling things you'll never get out of your head. Never. You just ... what you have left is each other. What you have are the men around you. You have the Marines who have your back no matter the cost to themselves. And you've got theirs. You'd lay down your life for any one of them, because you know they'd do the same for you. So, you never leave a man behind."

He pushed a plate of food in front of her and Mia was surprised to see he'd finished cooking while he talked. She'd been wholly caught up in his words and hadn't realized he had kept his hands going with food prep the whole time.

"Your dad got left behind somehow. I don't know how it

happened. It was like his body had come out, but somehow the rest of him was left behind. He needed someone to go in and grab him and bring his ass out." He shrugged. "So I did."

Mia looked down at her plate as her eyes blurred at the thought of her dad being left behind. She got what Jax was saying. Her dad had come home from the war, but something had been broken in him and it was a lot more than his leg. All her life, she'd thought of herself as the one who'd been abandoned, left behind. It hadn't occurred to her that maybe her dad had really been the one left behind.

She pushed the eggs around.

"Eat." Jax didn't wait for her to respond. He began eating his own food and didn't seem to care if she talked to him or not.

"He named me after the man who carried him four miles to safety and medical care when he was injured. My name was Michaela when I was born."

"It's not anymore?"

"No." She tasted the eggs now and had to bite back a sigh at the amount of butter the man had used. They were delicious and she had a feeling the toast would taste just as good. He'd laid the butter on thick there as well. She didn't know how he could eat like this without gaining a ton. When she cooked for herself, she cut out half the yolks and used olive oil and Herbs de Provence instead of butter. Hers tasted wonderful, too, but there was just something sinful and decadent about really buttery eggs and toast.

"My mom said people kept mistaking me for a boy when they saw my name, but I think in a way maybe it was my mom's way of fighting back after my dad left, even though it was years later when she changed my name. For a long time, she seemed like she was trying to fight off his memory somehow. She'd still tell me about him, tell me he was a good Marine and I should be proud of him, but I'd hear her crying at night in her room. She dated one guy for a long time and they even got engaged, but he left one day. They'd started fighting a lot. I think he knew she still loved my dad."

Mia bit her lip, realizing she had completely veered off the topic of her name and how it had been changed.

Reading her mind, Jax pushed her back on track. "And your name?" He set his plate down and leaned back against the sink.

"She changed it officially when I was seven. It says Mia on my birth certificate."

"I didn't know you could do that."

"She had to petition the court, but I guess the judge gave my mom discretion and allowed it. She told him my dad wasn't in the picture, so ..." she shrugged.

Mia's phone buzzed and she glanced at the screen.

Back soon?

It was her mom. She pushed off the bar stool she'd been sitting on and wiped her mouth with her napkin. "I'm sorry, that's my mom. I really need to get going."

"Come on," Jax said, following her toward the den, "I'll drive you back to the hotel.

"Oh, you don't need to do that." She looked down at the heels she'd worn the night before. No wonder her feet were sore. She hadn't exactly been dressed for walking.

Jax gave her a look and she knew there wouldn't be any arguing with him. He grabbed his keys and held the door for her. "You took a real risk walking over here in the middle of the night, by the way." There was no *by the way* about his tone. "That wasn't smart."

"Yeah. I don't think I've been all that smart about a lot

of things lately," Mia mumbled as she crossed the porch toward his driveway and the waiting Jeep.

As she got in, her phone rang.

"I'm sorry, mom," she said as she put the phone to her ear. "I'm on my way right now. Jax is dropping me off in just a minute."

As soon as she said the words, she realized her mom would want to know why she was with Jax and what they'd been doing all night. *Great.* Not very smart was the understatement of the century.

CHAPTER 13

"DETECTIVE?" The small nurse who'd shown him into the employee break room to wait for the doctor now gestured to him. "Let me show you to Dr. Coleman's office. He's waiting for you."

Jarrod nodded and stood. He'd told Chad's friend he would swing by and talk to the doctor, and he'd had some free time this morning.

The nurse knocked before opening a nondescript door and letting Jarrod enter, while she remained in the hallway. He understood why immediately. The room was tiny. Filing cabinets lined one side of the room and a medium-sized desk filled the rest of the space. There was room for a single chair in front of it.

"Good morning, detective," said a balding man in doctor's scrubs. He ran a hand over his head, as though his fingers itched to run through the hair that no longer existed on its crown. "What can I do for you?"

"I'm just here hoping you can give me some information on a former patient of yours. It's nothing, really." He threw the comment out there, sitting in the chair and drawing an air of casualness over him.

"Uh," the doctor hesitated, and rightfully so. Patients had rights.

"I'm sorry. I should clarify. The patient is deceased." Before he could continue, the doctor held up his hand.

"I'm sure you understand, detective, that the confidentiality still exists even after a patient's death. I'm afraid I can't share any information with you without a warrant."

Jarrod nodded. "I do, doctor. I appreciate where you're coming from. Here's the thing, though. I understand you can waive that confidentiality when there's a social need or safety concern or some such." He played it up for the doctor, as though he didn't know for sure what the law was. Jarrod was very familiar with the American Medical Association's recommended guidelines on this issue. "It's just that, a patient's medicine has been stolen, and I want to be sure we don't need to go hunting it down. All I want to do is try to be sure we don't have something really dangerous floating around out there."

The truth was, they had a lot of really dangerous substances floating around out there. Prescription drugs of all kinds could be bought and sold on a number of street corners in the city. But he hoped it would be enough to get the doctor talking.

If he wasn't mistaken, the doctor paled. Jarrod plowed on. "The patient was Leo Kent. I understand you're aware he died? That he was transferred from your clinic to the hospital?"

The doctor definitely paled at that. He was very aware of who Leo Kent was. "Yes. It was horrible. Not something that happens often, thankfully, but certainly something we have to be prepared for, nonetheless."

"And were you?"

"Were we what?"

"Prepared for it?" At this point, Jarrod wanted the doctor talking. He'd steer him around to where he needed to be later, but for the moment, simply talking was all he needed.

"Oh, yes."

The man didn't expand on the statement, and Jarrod sensed the doctor's hesitation. He didn't want him to stop the conversation all together. He decided to abandon the attempt to get Coleman to talk more about Leo, and honed in instead on the medication.

"So, what can you tell me about the medication Leo was taking? Is this something I need to be worried about getting out there on the streets, Doc?"

The hand went back to the doctor's almost nonexistent hair and Jarrod hoped the doctor didn't play poker.

"No, uh, I don't think so. I'll be honest with you, detective." Again, the hand ran front to back over the dome. "I gave Leo some sample sleep aids and pain killers. He wasn't really ill. He'd been having a lot of discomfort in his residual limb. You know he was an amputee?" He paused and looked to Jarrod, who nodded. "Anyway, he'd been having some pain lately and hadn't been sleeping well. We're not supposed to do it, clinic policy and all that, but I felt bad for the guy. I gave him some samples."

"What kind of samples?"

The doctor looked nervous, that hand going to the head again. "Pain meds. Sleeping pills."

"I see." Jarrod watched the doctor for a minute, before asking, "Is there any possibility those medications could have contributed to the heart attack he suffered, doctor?"

The doctor reddened and for a minute Jarrod thought

the man was going to explode. Then he simply looked defeated and shook his head. "No more so than if I'd written him a prescription and he took them inappropriately. If he took too many of them, combined them with alcohol, then yes. But I didn't get the sense he was doing any of that when he came in to the clinic that morning. He was coherent, he was seeking regular medical treatment."

Jarrod wasn't sure how much he should push the doctor to speak to him. Technically, the doctor was now on the edge of violating his patient's rights. "What was he complaining of when he came in that morning?"

He saw the doctor's hesitation, but it didn't last long. "He'd been tired and not feeling well, overall, for several days, but when he came in that morning, he thought he was experiencing heartburn."

"Heartburn? He mistook chest pain for heartburn."

"No. He was having pain in his upper abdomen, so he thought it was heartburn. I saw it for what it was. A heart attack often presents as chest pain, but people can also feel pain somewhere else in the body. Some feel it in their back, others the neck or jaw. His was presenting in the abdomen."

"So you sent him to the hospital?"

"No, we called for an ambulance. He was in no shape to make it there on his own. He collapsed just as they arrived. They were able to get an AED on him right away, but it was still too late."

"AED?" Jarrod asked.

"Automated External Defibrillator." The doctor shifted in his seat. "You said someone stole his medication?"

"Yes. Any ideas about that?" Jarrod had his own ideas but he wanted to see what the doctor thought.

Dr. Coleman shook his head. "I'm afraid what comes to mind is that he was selling the meds I gave him. Either that or he just told someone about them and that person heard about his death and decided to act."

Jarrod nodded. That had been his immediate thought, too, and knowing he'd had pain medication and sleeping aids firmed up that theory. He stood. "Well, doctor, thank you for your time."

"Anytime, detective." The doctor stood as well and Jarrod got the distinct feeling he couldn't wait for Jarrod to leave. That was understandable, he supposed, given the fact he'd been doling out medical samples he wasn't supposed to. There wasn't anything against the law about that, though, unless they were given out by someone who didn't have the authority to prescribe meds.

As Jarrod walked back to the parking lot, he answered a call from his partner.

"What's up, Cal?"

"I talked to the uniforms we had canvassing over at Leo Kent's apartment. They found one neighbor who saw someone leaving the apartment."

"Useful description?"

"Not the best I've ever heard, but not awful. One things stands out. She said the man was huge. Big linebacker kind of guy is how she described him. Sound like someone we know?"

"Hell yeah. That backs what the doctor just told me." Jarrod and Cal were both familiar with Carlos Perez, a street dealer known for pushing prescription meds, among other things. He certainly fit the woman's description.

"What's that?"

"He gave Leo sleeping pills and pain meds."

"Shit. So we think he was selling his meds to Carlos and word got out when he died?"

"Yeah, I figure if he was selling his meds, someone heard

about it and broke in to get whatever might be left. I wouldn't put that past Carlos," Jarrod said, starting the car. He sat and let the car run while they talked. "I'm headed to the station now. I'll meet you there and we can track down Carlos?"

"You got it."

Jarrod hung up, then dialed his phone again. He wasn't thrilled with what he had to tell Jaxon Cutter about Leo Kent, but he believed in getting the shit work done right away.

* * *

Jax wondered for a minute if he should have told Mia about the break-in at her dad's apartment as he watched her walk to the elevators in the hotel lobby. He felt guilty as hell for keeping it from her.

Combine that with the guilt he was feeling for fantasizing about her being in his bed all damned night, and he was feeling like shit. She was Leo's daughter *and* she was dating someone. The only problem was, she had his body screaming *go, go, go* when what he needed to be doing was saying *no, no, no*.

"What the hell is wrong with you?" He asked aloud. He didn't have an answer. It had taken all his control not to ask if he could see her again, but he'd clamped down on that urge and let her go.

The phone rang, giving him a reprieve. He hit the phone button on the steering wheel.

"Hello?"

"Hey, Jax. It's Jarrod Harmon."

Jax pulled into a gas station and took one of the parking spots on the side of the small building. He lifted his phone out of the dock it sat in on his dashboard and hit transfer before putting it to his ear

"Hi Jarrod. I didn't expect to hear from you so soon." That wasn't exactly true. He hadn't been a bit sure he'd hear back from the detective at all. There wasn't really much the detective could do about the break in at Leo's. Leo was gone and all that seemed to be missing were some meds. Not even a whole lot of them, at that.

"Well, I had some time this morning so I drove by the clinic and talked to Dr. Coleman." Jarrod filled him in on what they'd found so far. "I don't think much will come of it, but we're always glad to have the chance to go talk to this dealer, see if we can catch him with anything that might get him off the streets for a little while."

"Huh." Jax didn't really know what to say. It made sense that the doctor would be nervous about breaking the clinic's policy. "So you think someone just broke in to grab the meds? Why wouldn't they have taken the TV, or tossed the place for cash?"

"I don't know. We got a description from the neighbor and it sounds like a dealer we've dealt with before. If it is him, he wouldn't want the hassle of the television. He'd just want what he has ready buyers for: drugs."

Jax mulled it over and thought about the money Leo had tried to give him and the money he'd been sending Mia. *Shit*, he really didn't want to think Leo had been selling meds on the street. If it was true, it also meant Leo had flat out lied to him about picking up work.

"Thanks for looking into it, Jarrod." His gut churned with the idea that Leo had done that, but he guessed it didn't matter. The issue was as dead as Leo.

Then why did Jax still feel that fucking buzzing at the back of his neck?

"Anytime. Jax. Let me know if you need anything else."

Jax drove back to his place and quickly changed out his walking leg for his runner and put a matching running shoe on his other leg. He grabbed his earbuds and hit the road. He was glad he'd gotten in to see his prosthetist for an adjustment. If he ran long and hard enough, he could quiet his mind. And until then, he'd just drown out his thoughts.

He cranked Metallica and focused on the slow burn in his thighs.

CHAPTER 14

COLEMAN'S HANDS shook as he dialed the phone. He'd told the clinic staff he wasn't feeling well and had to leave, which left them short a doctor for the day.

Pacing the length of his home office wasn't helping and the damned man wasn't answering any of his calls. The old man probably spent half his damned day out on the golf course. He smashed the end button with his thumb and threw the phone on his desk.

He'd almost pissed his pants when that cop had walked into his office. The phone rang just as he was shoving three more antacids in his mouth. Not that they did any good.

"I've been trying to reach you for an hour. Where the hell have you been?" He was tempted to yell, but he couldn't risk his wife overhearing this conversation and asking questions.

The response didn't sound at all bothered. "In my lab. I do have work to do. Were you under the impression I sat by the phone waiting for your calls all day?"

Coleman ignored the scientist's sarcasm. "A police

detective showed up at the clinic. Did you have someone go to Leo Kent's place and take the medicine?"

"Of course I did. We can't have this stuff floating around out there for anyone to find."

"Well, they came to question *me* about it." Coleman sat in his desk chair, then popped back up and crossed to the window again.

There was silence on the other end of the phone for a moment so Coleman continued. "They wanted to know what I'd given him."

"And?"

"I told them I gave him some samples of sleeping pills and pain killers from one of my reps."

"Good. Problem solved."

Coleman exploded. "Not problem solved! Not problem solved at all. This isn't what I signed up for, damn it. I'm not doing this anymore. I can expose you, let the whole world know what you're doing."

The shift from bored to stone cold anger in the man's voice came through the phone loud and clear. "You'll keep it up until I tell you we're finished, Dr. Coleman. Don't forget what you're up against. If I stop making your payments, do you think the Genesios will simply forgive the debt?"

"I'll deal with the Genesios myself," Coleman bluffed. He didn't know how he would do that, but he'd figure something out. When they'd begun this, Coleman had believed in the drug they were creating. He'd wanted to help people as much as he'd wanted the money that had been offered.

His own brother and father had died of heart disease far too young. Perfecting this drug could mean other families wouldn't have to go through what his had been through. The pain of seeing life cut far too short for no good reason.

But people were dying because of the drugs they were doling out and he couldn't ignore what he was seeing now. He could see so clearly that this man had no interest in the science of this. There was something else at play here. He didn't know what the hell it was, but he couldn't sit by and let people continue to die.

"Do that and all this lands on your head."

The words shocked him, slamming into his brain with the force of a truck. "What the hell is that supposed—"

The man didn't let him finish. "It means I've got plenty of evidence that you were behind the drug trial. I've got logs of you visiting the lab at Simms Pharmaceutical"

"What the hell are you talking about? I never stepped foot in the lab when I went to Simms Pharmaceutical. I've never even seen the lab side of the facility. I've only been there to visit Warrick Staunton!"

"Of course you have. The logs reflect it. The police won't have any reason to think I was involved. In fact, why would they look at me at all when you and Warrick are the ones who are *old college buddies*? Add in your father and brother's deaths from heart failure and you have all the motive in the world to work with Warrick on this."

Coleman ground his teeth together. How on earth could this man have falsified the logs at Simms?

Of course he could. The man was mad, but he was also well-connected. He could likely make anything happen if he set his mind to it.

Suddenly it all made sense. The connection to Warrick, the resentment and history between the two men. This wasn't about the drug at all.

Coleman swallowed and hedged, trying to figure out where this was all headed. "Why on earth would the police think Warrick was involved?"

Warrick Staunton was a good man. He and Coleman had gone to undergrad together and shared a house their third and fourth years together with a couple of other guys. Coleman couldn't let this fall in his lap. "The police have no reason to think Warrick is involved."

As he said the words he realized they weren't true. Evidence could be planted far too easily. His stomach sank. He was so far into this shit, he would never get out.

"Jesus, are you testing the Simms drug that failed? People died during those trials!" Coleman couldn't believe this guy could be that crazy, but there wasn't any other explanation. He had to have known this would kill people before they'd even begun. "You can't possibly think you can bring it to market."

"Get yourself together and get your head back in the game, Dr. Coleman, or your friend Warrick will be left holding the bag." He sounded almost cheerful.

The call ended as Coleman sank into his desk chair again. The same question repeated in his head again and again.

How the hell had he gotten here?

CHAPTER 15

"HOLD UP, JAX." Jax looked to his left as Chad approached.

The two fell into step together as they walked toward the conference room at the end of the hall for the weekly tech and sci guy meeting. Logan's wife, Samantha, had deemed Jax's group at Sutton *the tech and sci guys*, and everything they did now was labeled that way. Including the weekly meetings.

"Was Jarrod able to help you out?" Chad asked, holding the conference room door for Jax. Kaeden was already sitting at the table, coffee and laptop arranged in front of him. Kaeden was always the first to get to their meetings.

"Yeah. Well, nothing came of it, but he looked into it for me." Jax turned toward the coffee setup at the side of the room and walked that way. Not that he needed the fix, but he wanted to tell Chad what Jarrod suspected quietly. It still killed him to think of Leo selling meds.

Chad followed and helped himself to a cup of coffee as well. "Everything okay?"

"Yeah." Jax glanced over his shoulder, but Kaeden was

in his own world, analyzing something intently on his computer screen. "He went and saw the doctor to see what Leo might have had in the apartment. Turns out the doctor had given him some sleeping pills. He was also on pain meds for his leg. I'd taught him mirror therapy and that was working well for him, so I'm not sure why he would need pain meds."

"Mirror therapy?"

"It's a pretty new thing for amputees. If you have an amputated leg, you put a mirror between your legs, facing the intact leg. You do exercises and massage with it and watch in the mirror. I don't know how the hell it does it, but somehow your brain seems to process it as the other leg doing the exercises. Cuts down on the pain a ton."

"No shit?"

Jax nodded. Mirror therapy had been a Godsend for him when he'd first lost his limb. "Jarrod thinks he might have been selling the pills and whoever he was selling them to broke in to grab the rest of his stash after he died."

Chad shook his head. "I'm sorry, man."

Jax nodded, mouth tight. He hated the feeling of bitter disappointment he felt. What right did he have to judge Leo? Leo had his reasons for doing what he did.

In fact, if Leo was selling medications the doctor had given him, it wasn't lost on Jax that *he* might have been part of Leo's reasons for doing what he'd done.

Jax had pressured Leo into accepting money from him to rent that apartment. Maybe Leo didn't want to feel like he was in debt to Jax forever. Maybe he'd just been trying to get out from under that debt, even though Jax hadn't ever intended that Leo pay him back.

Chad clapped him on the shoulder as the room began to fill with the others on their team. Sara Blackwell and

Samantha walked in together and all talk turned to the new prosthesis on Sara's arm. The two had been inventing detachable tools for prosthetic arms using Sara as the guinea pig.

Being at work sucked lately. He'd liked his job and had been starting to feel closer to this group, in particular. Most of the people in the room were either former military or spouses of former military. They worked well together.

Lately, though, nothing seemed to work as far as Jax was concerned. It had been over a week since he'd dropped Mia off at the hotel the day after Leo's funeral, and all he thought about was either her or the fact that things still didn't sit right with him as far as Leo was concerned.

Jax and Chad wandered over to join the group as Sara grinned and showed off the newest tool she and Sam had come up with. She had a socket style prosthesis base with several attachments she was putting in and out to show the group. She'd just plugged a whisk in to demo.

"It's our kitchen set," she said with a laugh. She and Samantha had been putting together camping sets, an arts and crafts set, a set for a tattoo artist. They were talking to a jeweler who wanted to have some specially made tools.

Jax picked up one of the attachments. It was a six-inch chef's knife. "What happens when your kid comes in the room and startles you when you're using this?"

"How's that any different from a kid startling their mom who's holding a knife?"

He shrugged. "I don't know. Maybe it's not."

He sat back, fidgeting with the handle of his coffee cup as he waited for the meeting to start, but his mind wandered again. He wondered if Mia was having trouble settling in at work, or if her father's death was plaguing her. Of course, she still didn't know about the break in or the medicines. Jax had zero interest in telling her now that he knew what Leo was likely doing for money.

"Jax ... Jax? You still with us?" Sam's voice cut in.

"Huh? Oh yeah, sorry. Zoned out. What did you say?"

Chad looked at him sideways. "You sure you're okay?"

"Yeah, I'm good. Just tired." Jax brushed off the question and pulled out his tablet. He was supposed to be updating the group on some of the figures from a company they'd been vetting over the last month.

"I asked if you wanted to play basketball tonight. We're meeting up after work and Jack can't make it. The kids are sick."

Jax raised his brows, but Chad waved a hand "Nothing major. Stomach bug. Not fun for him or Kelly, but the kids will probably be bouncing off the wall again by morning. So, can you make it? We're short one."

"Sorry. I'm meeting with the super to give him back Leo's keys and get the security back and all that."

"That sucks. Hey, Kaeden, you interested?"

As the conversation moved on around him, Jax thought about the medals he had from Leo's apartment back at his place. He needed to pack them up and send them up to Mia's mom.

Or maybe he'd just drive them up to Mia's office and drop them off in person.

Idiot. He was a complete idiot. He needed to forget about Mia Kent and get on with his life.

CHAPTER 16

JAX LOOKED around the area surrounding the homeless shelter and clinic. Between the two buildings was a courtyard with quiet benches and a surprisingly serene garden. A plaque in one corner read:

Victoria Tyvek Staunton
Loving Daughter
Taken Too Soon
1980-2013

Across the street from the shelter, things were less tranquil. A parking lot and overpass created an area ripe for the shelter's overflow to stay.

When he'd first met Leo, the place had been a lot more crowded than it was now. The initiatives happening in Connecticut with the homeless were really making a difference in the lives of a lot of people. Now, the shelter saw a lot of business for job training and counseling, and the clinic was still swamped, but they had less use of their emergency beds.

The streets weren't entirely empty, though. There were still men and women of all ages sitting on stoops or standing in the parking lot adjacent to the building. He guessed the people who slept at the shelter didn't always have somewhere to go during the day. Or they might be waiting for appointments at the shelter itself in job training and support services offered during daytime hours.

Jax walked toward the overpass across the street, where he'd spent time with Leo and some of the other veterans who lived on New Haven's streets. He hadn't been down here since Leo had moved into the apartment and it struck Jax that he should have kept up his visits. He could be doing more to help other people who were on the streets.

He spotted a woman in a shadowed corner of the area, her heavy coat covering what seemed to be layers of clothing. Darla always wore layers and he wondered for a minute if she was sweating her ass off, but he knew the struggle. If she got rid of layers now, she'd have to find a safe place to stash them or risk losing them when it turned cold. She'd rather keep the layers on than be stuck out in the cold without.

"Hey Darla," he said quietly, keeping his distance. Most of the time she was in the mood to talk, but he'd seen her when she wasn't. He could respect that. He had been a little surprised not to see her and Jimmy at the funeral.

The older woman turned wary eyes to him, but brightened when she saw him. "Leo's boy."

The men and women he'd met from Leo's life all called him Leo's boy, as if he'd been his son. Now that he knew Mia existed it made him a little uncomfortable. He knew it had to suck for her to know Jax and Leo had had the relationship she'd craved all her life.

"Jax," he said, smiling. "Do you mind if I sit?" He

gestured to the concrete next to her and she nodded her assent.

He looked around. "Where's Jimmy?"

"Gone," she sniffed, and Jax realized her eyes were tearing up. "He died just over a month back."

"I'm so sorry, Darla. I hadn't heard." He wondered if Leo had known. If he had, he hadn't mentioned it to Jax.

He didn't know if Darla and Jimmy had been married or just long time partners, or friends or what. But he hadn't ever seen one without the other.

"Same as Leo. Heart attack." She turned and looked at him fiercely. "It was those meds."

She dug into the pocket of her coat and pulled out an empty pill bottle. It was the plastic amber kind you'd get in any pharmacy across the country but there was no label, and no evidence there'd ever been one. "Damned pills."

She looked at the bottled and Jax could see the agony of her loss. He wished he was better at this. That he could think of something to say to take away her ache.

Jax realized one of Leo's pill bottles hadn't had a label. He hadn't thought much of it at the time, but it sure as hell got his attention now. "What were the pills for?"

She looked at him, and for a minute she looked like she'd forgotten he was there. Then she seemed to remember, and answered him. "The clinic. They said he had to take those pills for them, but then he got sick, and they wouldn't help him."

"He was taking the pills *for* the clinic?" Jax wondered if she was talking about a drug trial.

"Right up until he died. Heart attack, they said." She shook her head and hissed. "That's what they say, but he was strong as an ox, my Jimmy. No heart attack gonna take him from me. It was those pills."

Jax looked at the empty bottle. "Do you mean a drug trial, Darla?"

She nodded. "Yes. For the drug trials. That's it."

"Can I take that?" He pointed to the pill bottle and she drew it back away from him, cradling it to her. He raised his hands. "I just thought I could take it to a friend of mine. He's a detective with the NHPD. I could ask him to look into this. It might help if he had the bottle."

Jax had no clue if the bottle would be helpful to Jarrod but he wanted to get as much information as he could. Who knew. Maybe they could swab the inside of the bottle and see what it had held. His gut wasn't going to stop screaming until they had answers.

Maybe the doctor was telling the truth, and Leo had been selling drugs. But Darla's story had him wondering just how much of their current theory was bullshit.

She nodded slowly and turned over the bottle. He pocketed it. "Thank you. Can I find you down here again if I need to Darla, or is there some way I can get ahold of you?"

"I'll be here. I'm always here." She began to stand but he stopped her. "Here, Darla. Get some lunch, okay?"

He handed her a lot more than a lunch's worth of cash, and she smiled but there was deep sorrow engraved in the lines of her face. He wondered how long she would last without Jimmy and hoped she had other people she could lean on out here. He'd need to see if he could talk to someone at the shelter about her. Maybe help get her into an apartment.

It made him sad to think that she was living on the streets with no support. People shouldn't have to grow old out here. If his mom was out here alone—Jesus, the thought killed him. Darla could be someone's mom, too. Was there someone out there worrying about her? Wondering where she was and if she was alive?

Jax thought again of what she'd just told him. He didn't know much about drug trials, but he would guess there was no way in hell they should be giving out unmarked bottles of pills to anyone. If Leo wasn't the only one to have had a heart attack, maybe Jax wasn't making more out of this than there really was. Either way, he needed to find out. He owed Leo.

CHAPTER 17

MIA CURLED her feet up under her and sipped the lemonade her mom had put in front of her. The back porch of her mom's house was one of her favorite places to be. They had a tradition of sitting on the back porch swing sipping lemonade as they talked in the evenings. It was where they'd always ended up for all of the important talks in Mia's life. The breakups, fights with girlfriends, decisions about where to go to college.

"So," her mother said, and Mia had a feeling she'd been lured here this evening for something other than lemonade and a light chat. "Have you seen Jax again?"

Mia nearly choked on her lemonade as her cheeks flushed. "Jax? Mom, I told you. It wasn't like that when I spent the night."

Her mom shrugged. "But there's no reason it couldn't be."

At times, her mom could seem more like a friend than her mom, but she suspected that came from being an only girl raised by a single mom. Her father's parents had blamed her mother when their son slipped off the grid. She hadn't known them at all as a child or an adult.

Her mother's mom had died when her mom was a teen. Her grandfather on her mom's side had been part of Mia's life until she was ten, but then he'd passed away. It struck Mia sometimes, how alone in the world she and her mom were.

Mia narrowed her eyes at her mom. "Of course there's a reason there can't be anything between Jax and me." She wasn't about to admit to her mom that she'd thought about Jax every day since the funeral.

"What's the problem? He's a handsome man with a good job."

There were so many problems, Mia didn't know where to begin. Jax was tied to her father in Mia's mind and her emotions were all over the map as far as that went. She resented him for having been able to know her dad in a way she hadn't. She resented the fact that he seemed to think her dad could do no wrong, when in fact, he'd done a lot of wrong. Leo had walked away from her and her mom. There was no more wrong a man could do, as far as she was concerned.

"Have you forgotten about Nick?" She frowned at her mom. "I'm already dating someone, who also happens to be a handsome man with a good job."

Her mom made a dismissive noise and waved her hand.

"Mom!" Mia couldn't believe her mom. "I thought you liked Nick."

"I do like him. But I'm surprised I need to point out to you that you and Nick are really nothing more than friends who kiss sometimes."

"What! What on earth does that mean, mom?"

"It means it's heading nowhere. I know you. You're

hiding out with Nick."

Her mom wrapped an arm around her and squeezed. I know what happened with Gary scared you. It scared me." Mia's mom had been there with her when Gary began stalking her, becoming possessive and jealous. Dangerous.

"What happened with your dad, what happened with Gary. I think both of those things have combined to make you want to hide, whether you realize you're doing it or not. Nick is safe, but neither of you feels any passion for each other."

Mia blushed. Discussing the level of *passion* in her relationship was not at all something she wanted to do with her mom. Unfortunately, her mom seemed to have no qualms about it and plowed on forward.

"I'm not even sure you're really *good* friends. You're a good friend to *him*, but where was he during your father's funeral?"

Mia shifted in her seat. "I didn't ask him to come." In the past, he'd somehow been this safety net for her. Like an old sweatshirt that was familiar with its torn holes at the sleeves and elbows. But now she was starting to see that things weren't what they should be. Maybe her mom was right. Maybe he'd been more of a hideout than a safety net.

"He should have been there without being asked." Her mom didn't stop. "Jax was there for you that night."

"Shouldn't you want me to stay away from veterans?" The minute the words were out of Mia's mouth, she wanted to take them back.

"Oh, honey," her mom reached out and tugged a lock of her hair like she did when she was little. "I know this is hard for you to understand, but I don't regret falling in love with your dad. Even if the war did break something inside of him, I have no regrets for the time we did have together. I don't think I would do you any justice by making you avoid all men who've served in the military."

Mia sipped her drink, using it to avoid the conversation as she nudged the swing back and forth with one foot.

"I wish you'd had the chance to get to know your dad before he died." There was a thick quality to her mom's voice like she was fighting back tears and Mia hated herself for bringing her mom to that place.

Mia huffed. "I'm not sure if that would have been good or not. Maybe it's just better this way."

"Why do you say that?"

"I don't know. I just feel like I didn't have him here all this time and things were okay. Now, I've got this awful feeling that I can't quite cope with and I'm sad for a man I didn't know and confused about everything."

And wanting nothing more than to go see Jax again, which made her moody as hell. She liked him. A lot more than she should.

She debated how much to tell her mom. "My feelings for Jax are confusing. I think in a way they're sort of all twisted up in my feelings about dad." Not to mention the fact that she owed it to Nick to make a decision about their relationship before seeing Jax again.

"That makes sense, but I don't think you should let that get in the way of getting to know him."

Mia shifted away from thoughts and talk of Jax and asked the question she'd been putting off for too long.

"Why did he leave us, Mom?" It came out almost a whisper. It wasn't that she hadn't asked before, but it was a question she hadn't asked as an adult. As a child, her mom's answers had satisfied her to some degree. They'd been vague. As a teen, she'd learned to stop asking.

Now, she wanted the full story. The true reason she hadn't grown up with her dad.

A deep sigh came from her mom, but she put her arm around Mia and pulled her close. "Your father came back from his last deployment with injuries on both the inside and out. Something had broken inside of him."

Her mom paused as though reliving the history as she spoke.

"He began to drink. A lot. We fought. I wanted him to get more help. He said the therapists from the VA weren't helping him. That they couldn't help him."

Mia tried to picture what life would have been like for her mother and father then. She knew how much her mom loved her father, even after all this time. It must have torn her up to see him like that.

"One night, we argued." Her mom sounded resigned to telling the story now, but she shook her head. The movement was so slight Mia wasn't sure she was even aware of it, as though she could erase what had to be said before it reached Mia's ears. "It was worse than any other night. I thought—"

Her mom stopped and Mia was torn between telling her mom it was okay to keep the secret and needing to know what had happened.

A few deeps breaths later and her mom continued. "I thought he was going to hit me. He spun and it wasn't until after I'd taken a step backward that I realized he'd only been reaching his hands up in frustration. I could see it so clearly as I tumbled backward, the look of shock on his face. But it was too late."

Oh God. Dread filled Mia's stomach like acid and she didn't want to hear the rest.

"We were at the top of the steps. I stepped back over

them. Your dad tried to reach for me. He ran down the stairs and held me."

Her mom was crying and Mia had tears streaming down her face. "Oh mom."

"I was pregnant. Your dad called an ambulance, but I lost the baby. A boy."

Mia held her mom and closed her eyes.

"It destroyed your dad. He blamed himself. He said he couldn't ever take a chance on hurting either one of us again. It was a self-imposed exile, I suppose. A way to punish himself for something he saw as his fault, even though it was as much my fault as it was his."

She turned to Mia. "I need you to understand, your father had *never* laid a finger on me. He'd never hurt me. I don't know what made me think he would that night. Why I thought I needed to step back. He was drunk and angry, but I need you to believe me when I tell you, I knew as soon as it happened that he never intended to hurt me."

Mia nodded, her throat too thick to speak. A brother. She had a brother.

"I know that sounds like I'm making excuses for a man who abused me, but it isn't like that. He never once hurt me that way."

They sat without speaking for a long time. "I kept thinking he would come back. That he'd see reason and realize he wouldn't put us in danger if he came back. He never did. Your dad never came back because he never would have put you or me into a position where his demons could harm us again."

All Mia could think was how much they'd all paid for that night. For the fallout from one fight, one split second in time.

CHAPTER 18

NICK STARED at Mia and for the life of her she couldn't read his face. She couldn't decide if he looked annoyed, inconvenienced maybe?

"Is this about your dad? I told you I had to work. I would have been there if I could have been, Mia."

"No, Nick. I've just realized, I don't think we're right for each other. I don't feel what I should feel for you."

"I don't even know what that means."

Mia smiled sadly. She had a feeling he really didn't know what it meant. Her mother's words echoed in her head and she repeated them for him. "I don't feel any passion for you." She shook her head. "And I have a feeling you don't feel the way you should for me, either."

"So, what, you want me to kiss you more?" He looked frustrated now, but she had the sense again that this was more about a change to his plans than about missing her or wanting her in his life. Nick had a plan and a way he expected things to go in his life.

"No. What I want is for us both to find someone we're passionate about." She wasn't surprised when Jax filled her thoughts as she spoke. "I want us both to find someone who makes us feel—" she paused as she thought, but the words didn't take long to come. "Someone who makes you feel excited and happy every time you talk to them. Someone whose calls you can't wait to get. Who you can't wait to see and talk to." *To touch. To be touched by.*

She didn't tell him what else she was thinking. She didn't mention the way Jax made her feel like she was on fire with nothing more than the slightest touch of his hand. That he made her feel that thrill at the smallest of contact. Like there was so much more to come.

Nick's face clouded. "I see. You've already found someone who makes you feel this way."

"I have. It's not someone I'm involved with. I wouldn't do that to you, but it made me open my eyes to what we don't have between us." She took a deep breath. "I think we're better friends than we are lovers, Nick. I just didn't see that before."

* * *

Mia waited a week before going to see Jax. She was a little surprised she lasted that long. She'd been wrung out emotionally after hearing her mother and father's story. It had taken a lot of processing and a lot of tears to come to terms with what had happened.

And she was angry. Angry as hell at a system that had so completely dropped the ball for her dad. He'd fought for this country and suffered such an incredible breakdown when he came home.

She and her mom had talked long into the night about the times her dad had gone to the VA seeking help and not found what he needed. He'd been turned away and told to come back in a few days more times than her mom could count.

In some respects, her dad was lucky. He wasn't vilified the way Vietnam veterans were. The Gulf War was supported by the people. To many people, its soldiers were heroes when they arrived home. But that didn't change the fact that there weren't enough resources to help those soldiers cope with all they'd seen and done.

Now, standing in front of his door, Mia wondered if Jax was getting the support he needed. She wondered for a minute at the chance she was taking getting involved with him. If that's even what she was doing. She really didn't know.

But she'd be lying if she said she wasn't a little uncertain about getting involved with someone who shared the history and the struggles that had led her mom and dad to implode years before.

She knocked on the door anyway, unable to turn back now.

Jax opened the door almost immediately, and met her eyes. They stood watching one another a long moment before he put one hand out to pull her into his chest and hold her tight to him.

She didn't know what had sparked the gesture, but she didn't care. His arms felt so good around her. He was strong and comforting in a way she needed so badly at that moment. She leaned into his hold and breathed deep, letting the clean scent she'd come to associate with him fill her senses.

After a minute, he pulled back and looked her in the eye again. "You okay?"

"I broke up with Nick." She hadn't meant to blurt that out and didn't have any idea why she'd said it.

Jax's eyebrows went up, but he didn't say anything.

"That's not why I'm here, though. I had a brother." Tears began to fall again as she told him the story of her younger brother and how his life was lost.

At some point, Jax pulled her to the couch, settling her in next to him as she talked.

"I wish you'd had the chance to know your dad before he died," he said when she finished. "He had managed to heal a lot in all this time. I imagine he never got over the guilt of what happened that night or the guilt of leaving you and your mom, but he was a different man than the one your mom is describing."

"You said you struggled when you came back, too. Was it really bad for you?" She threaded her fingers through his as she asked the question and looked down at their intertwined hands.

"Not nearly as bad as what your mom described. I had nightmares for a while. I still do sometimes. But the dreams didn't chase me during the day the way they do for some guys."

"Did you have a hard time with your injuries?"

He frowned, trying to think of a way to explain it to her. "Not really. Well, I guess yes and no. I had a lot of phantom pain and some frustration when I couldn't learn things as quickly as I wanted to. But, I was mostly relieved about the level of my injury. I wasn't angry about losing my leg. I think that made it easier. I was so freaking grateful to still be here."

He looked at her and she waited, knowing there was more. "I think I could have turned to alcohol or even pain meds, if I hadn't met a few really good people along the way."

"Like who?" She found she wanted to know more and

more about him.

"Your dad, for one. And a doctor who helped me with the pain of the amputation without needing the pain meds all the time."

"I'm glad you had them to help you."

"Me, too," he said quietly. "Now tell me what happened with Nick."

Mia's cheeks flamed. "Sorry. I really didn't mean to blurt that out."

He raised an eyebrow and waited.

"I just realized we weren't really right for each other. I think I've actually known that for a while now, but I've been doing everything I could to avoid really facing it."

"Why is that?"

"It was comfortable. Safe." She felt her heart racing as they talked and realized Jax made her feel anything but that. Well, that wasn't entirely true. She certainly felt safe with him. But she also felt the excited rush of being with someone who made her really feel things. She had that feeling of not being able to really catch her breath around him. Of waiting and hoping he'd kiss her. Touch her. Of wanting to be back in his arms again.

She didn't mention what had happened with Gary years before. She'd tell him about it eventually, but not now.

"How did he take it?"

She laughed. "There wasn't crying and pleading, that's for sure. Annoyed is mostly how I would put it. We really weren't right for each other. I think his pride was hurt, but I have a feeling he'll see that I'm right soon, if he hasn't already."

"Were you together long?" She got the sense he was

trying to gauge how much space to give her, or maybe the length of rebound time she might need.

She shook her head slowly at him. "Six months."

Jax reached for her and pulled her closer, tugging her legs over his lap and drawing her into his arms. "I really hated that guy," he said and his voice took on a deliciously gruff tone.

Mia laughed, but she could hear the breathlessness in it. "You never met him."

"Didn't matter," he said, before he kissed her and all thought left her. His mouth on hers was everything she never knew she wanted. It was demanding and powerful, but somehow soft at the same time. Her whole body felt instantly needy for him.

She wrapped her arms around his shoulders and was shocked to feel herself pull him closer. *More*. That was all she could think, that she wanted more. More of the fluttery feeling he gave her. More of his hands on her body, his mouth on her mouth. Everything.

She lost herself in the feel of his body pressed to hers. He was all muscle beneath her. All hard, lean muscle that seemed to beg her hands to touch.

He seemed to keep his sanity better than she did because he drew back slowly, intense eyes locked on hers. "Sorry. Couldn't help myself."

She nodded, stupidly, too overwhelmed to say a word. The last thing she wanted to be thinking about at a time like this was her mom or her ex, but she couldn't help it.

Her mom had been right. There had been zero passion between her and Nick. He didn't come anywhere close to making her feel anything like this. Her body didn't hum with electricity when she was around him.

"You okay?" Jax asked, a hint of amusement in his tone.

"Yes," she said. There was that damned breathless thing again. She cleared her throat. "Fine. Good. Everything's great."

Now he laughed and she realized she hadn't heard him laugh like that yet. It was deep and full, like he was holding nothing back. She liked that about him. He seemed comfortable with himself.

"How about I take you out for dinner?"

"You didn't have plans?" She asked. She had just crashed his evening, after all.

"Nope. Nothing to do but spoil you." He stood and tugged her off the couch. "Although you probably do need to do something about this." He grinned and waved his hands around her face and hair.

Now it was her turn to laugh. She probably looked awful. She'd just cried on his shoulder for half an hour. "Bathroom?"

"Down that hall, second door on the right," he said, walking behind her, one hand on her back as they moved together down the hall.

Mia stopped laughing when she looked in the mirror. She was giving new meaning to the smoky eye look. She took a tissue and smeared at the eyeliner. At least she was wearing waterproof mascara. Her hair was mussed and her cheeks stained from her tears, and he still wanted to take her out to dinner. Good to know.

She did her best to straighten her hair and walked out.

Her breath caught as she left the room. Jax stood, leaning against the wall waiting for her. He'd put on a char-coal button down shirt and the look in his eyes tempted her to stay in rather than go out. He seemed to set her on fire with just those eyes.

He held out a strong hand. "Ready?"

"Yes." She took his hand and felt her stomach flip. It wasn't a bad flip. It was the kind of excitement that meant something new and big and probably not like anything she'd ever experienced was about to start. And she would bet anything it wouldn't end with them as friends who sometimes kissed.

CHAPTER 19

JAX PICKED Mia up at her house for their second official date. The hour long drive to Hartford wasn't exactly ideal for a dinner date, but he didn't care. He liked her. A lot.

He'd given up on trying to talk himself out of being with her. Yes, she was Leo's daughter. And, yeah, he wasn't completely sure he was ready to be with a woman. But he'd like to think Leo would give them his blessing. In fact, Leo probably would have told Jax he was being an idiot if he walked away from a woman he liked this much. Who made him feel the way she did.

He damned near choked on his own tongue when she opened the door. A bright red sweater framed her shoulders, leaving the tops of them bare and her neck exposed.

He didn't see what she wore on the bottom. He couldn't look away from the silken skin above her collar bone.

He wanted nothing more than to start at the top and work his way down, licking and nibbling his way as she moaned in his ear.

"Hi," she said and he could tell from the question in her

voice she was wondering why he was standing there staring at her without saying a word.

He blew out a breath. "You look gorgeous," he said, though it came out a bit rough and he cleared his throat.

Her smile was slow and sweet. "You do, too," she said, and he could see she meant it.

All the nerves over being with a woman flew out the window and he wondered why he'd been worried. Mia had never once made him feel uncomfortable about his leg. What would make him think she'd change any when their clothes came off?

If their clothes came off. He was jumping the gun a little.

Not hard to do with how she made him feel, but still probably not a good idea to get ahead of himself.

He cleared his throat again and put out his hand for her. "Ready?"

She slipped her small hand into his and walked out the door with him, pausing to lock up.

"Where are we headed?" she asked as he opened the Jeep door for her and gave her a hand in.

"How do you feel about Chinese?"

"Love it." She smiled at him and he felt like he'd won the lottery.

They had dinner and talked about where they'd grown up, siblings, school, all that. His large family was very different from hers. She'd grown up with just her mom and her, and her mother's father until he passed away. She had an aunt and uncle and a couple of cousins, but they were scattered around the country and she didn't see them often.

By contrast, he was close to his brothers, and even though his family had moved constantly based on where his father's post was, he and his brothers had often spent summers with their cousins. There had been endless months of running wild on his uncle's farm in Indiana. Stripping down to underwear to jump in the river or swinging from tire swings they'd rigged that might or might not hold their weight.

She told him about the jobs she'd worked to put herself through college. The list ranged from overnight clerk at an all-night photo development place, for the short stint the place was open, to bartender at a downtown Hartford dive. Apparently, there's not enough business to sustain an all-night photo development store, but she saw some pretty interesting pictures while she was there.

She laughed as she described some of her favorites. "This one guy came in with pictures of himself playing tennis in nothing but boxers and hiking boots."

"What?" Jax couldn't picture it. Hell, he wasn't sure he wanted to, but he also couldn't stop smiling as her eyes lit and she laughed.

"Yup. And then he asked us which one we thought was the best one to post on his online dating profile."

Jax didn't have a response for that.

Forty-five minutes later, he looked across the table at her. "I thought you said you love Chinese?"

"I do!"

"You hardly ate a thing," he said pulling the bowl of fried rice toward him for his third helping. The woman had eaten a small spoonful from each of the three entrees they'd ordered to split and a little scoop of the fried rice.

She laughed. "I'm not nearly your size, Jax. I can't eat a truckload of lo mein and top it off with three egg rolls, an order of General Tsao's chicken and two beers."

He shrugged and grinned at her. "I run a lot. It makes me hungry."

"I can't imagine your poor mom trying to cook for you and your brothers."

"She didn't."

"What?"

He laughed. "She's a horrible cook. I guess when we were little she cooked more, but when we were teens, we did a lot of the cooking. My brothers and I became masters of the grill."

"That's so funny. I had this picture in my head of your mom as this, I don't know, Susie Homemaker or something. Taking care of her big burly men."

He put down his fork and rested a hand on his now-full stomach. "She was, in a lot of ways. She was always there shuffling us from one sports practice to the next. And she was really active on whatever base we were stationed on at the time. She kind of held all the wives together when the stress of not knowing when your husband was coming home, or sometimes even where he was deployed, got to them. My mom was there for them. Always."

He took Mia's hand in his. "She just can't cook and has zero interest in learning. She was so bad at it that when my dad would come home, he'd tell her how much he wanted her to cook for him, but he didn't want to hurt our feelings by telling us not to barbecue. He played it up like it was this big deal to let his sons show him their grilling skills. She knew what he was doing, but everyone played along."

He laughed looking back and remembering his dad trying not to tell his mom he hated her cooking. "What about your mom? Does she cook?"

Mia smiled. "Yes. I don't know how she kept it all together. She'd work such crazy long hours, but she'd come home and make the best meals. Heavy stuff. I look back now and can't believe I didn't weigh a million pounds.

Pasta, fried chicken. She makes this amazing macaroni with hard boiled eggs and cheese. It sounds kind of gross, but it's so good. I still ask her for that one sometimes."

"I'm hungry just listening to that."

She was incredulous. "You're crazy. I don't know how you can think about eating after the meal you just ate."

He grinned back at her as the waitress handed him the check. He glanced at the bill and placed a credit card on it before placing it on the edge of the table. "Give me half an hour, I'll be ready to eat again."

CHAPTER 20

JARROD LOOKED over the top of his computer at Cal, who'd just walked back into the precinct with coffee for both of them. They'd developed a bad habit of going down the street to buy coffee from the Dunkin Donuts at Union Station. It was just so much better than the tar that was brewed in the station house that it made the walk worth it if they could afford the time to slip away.

Not to mention it got at least one of them up off their ass for a few minutes every few hours. Some days, the chance to get away from their desks was gold. Other days, they'd kill for the chance to sit down. A detective's day could vary drastically depending on their active cases.

Cal handed him one of the matching large cups of black coffee. The trip always took a few minutes longer when Cal was the one to take it. The man wouldn't leave the station house without putting on sunscreen unless it was a flat out, sirens blaring emergency.

"Thanks," Jarrod said. "I've got interesting news."

"Yeah, what's that?"

"Carlos couldn't be the guy our witness saw at Leo

Kent's place. Vice had him under surveillance the entire day. They've been watching him for a while now. Apparently, he's upped his game and they're interested in taking him out."

Cal bit out a curse. "Well, that blows that theory out of the water."

"Yeah, it does, but take a look at this." He turned the monitor so Cal could see the report he'd pulled up.

Cal grunted, but Jarrod had no trouble translating the sound.

"Yeah, weird, huh?"

"Go back a year." Cal gestured at the screen.

Jarrod resubmitted the form, plugging in all the same variables but taking it back another year in time.

Now both men grunted as they looked at the screen.

"Yeah. You show anyone this yet?"

"No. Figured we'd go talk to the captain when you got back." He grinned, knowing Cal wouldn't appreciate the fact he'd waited for him. Who wanted to bring something like this to the captain?

"You're a freaking prince."

Jarrod laughed and headed to the printer to pull the sheets he'd just printed. It looked like Jax Cutter had stumbled onto something after all.

* * *

"You were right."

Jax looked at the phone. *Jarrod.* He'd answered on autopilot and now had to orient himself. Mia's slight figure on top of him felt good. Damned good.

He and Mia had fallen asleep on her couch after watching a movie. Her hair tickled his nose as she sat up and he felt the warmth of her body leaving his. He looked at Mia, who blinked up at him. "Sorry," he said, and sat up, feeling her eyes on him.

"Hang on, Jarrod. I'm not awake yet. Just give me a second."

Mia walked into her kitchen and grabbed two bottles of water, handing one to him before walking back out of the room. Jax took a drink, then spoke into the phone. "Sorry. Go."

"You were right about the clinic. Something's up. Cal and I did some digging and we found a gradual uptick in the number of heart attacks where the victim died either in the shelter or clinic in the last four months. These last two months there were six."

"So six in two months counting Leo? That seems high," Jax said. He squinted at the clock on Mia's DVD player. Seven thirty in the morning.

"Well, that's the thing. It is and it isn't. No one thought much of it because on the whole, homeless people have a much higher rate of death in general, including deaths as a result of heart attack. Among homeless men, the rate of death from heart disease is nearly twice that for people who have housing."

"You're kidding. Jesus, that's crazy." The irony struck Jax. Leo had just gotten into a house, yet he'd still fallen victim to the shocking statistic.

"Yeah, I hadn't really expected those numbers. The thing is, we looked back at this shelter in particular, and it seems like this number of deaths in such a small time frame so closely linked to that one clinic is a bit odd. They average anywhere between zero and two heart attacks per month. The last two months there were six, and the month before that, four. It's not enough that we can open an official investigation, but enough that my captain said we could take a peek into it off the books and see if it's something we need to look into."

"Were you able to tell anything from that pill bottle?" Jax asked, keeping his voice low.

"Not sure yet. The lab swabbed it to see if they could find any residue and identify what was inside, but I doubt they'll find anything. As for fingerprints, there's nothing really useable. It's filled with smeared and partial prints that I suspect would only come up as Darla's. I don't know how long she was hanging onto that bottle, but it seems like she was using it as sort of a touchstone. Maybe to her, it was a connection to Jimmy," Jarrod said.

"So what next?"

"We'll talk to the ME about the other deaths. See what we can find out or if there was anything suspicious about them."

"The medical examiner?" asked Jax. "I don't think Leo's body even went to the city. The funeral home picked him up from the hospital morgue for cremation."

As he said it, he realized the enormity of that statement. Leo had been cremated. Any evidence would likely be gone.

Jarrod seemed to follow his train of thought. "Yeah. So, the way this works is if a person dies under the care of a physician and there's no evidence of foul play, as in the case of a heart attack, the doctor signs the death certificate and the ME doesn't take jurisdiction. If a body is found, though, then the ME takes jurisdiction and will, at the very least, perform a routine exam to determine cause of death. We'll try to find out what the circumstances were surrounding those deaths and see if the bodies have been claimed or what."

"You'll let me know?" Jax asked, wishing there was more he could do.

"As much as I can, yes. If the ME took possession of any of these bodies, she would have performed an autopsy and kept tissue and blood samples. We need permission to test those, though."

"I'm not sure if Darla was Jimmy's legal wife or if they were just together, or what," Jax said, his thoughts on next of kin.

"I'll see if I can find out."

Jarrod hung up and Jax stared at the closed kitchen door.

Jax didn't know how much he should tell Mia about her dad and the medicine and the fact that he was having Jarrod look into whatever it was that was going on. Part of him knew she had a right to know what was going on, but he also didn't want to mess with what was happening between them. He had a feeling telling her about all of this would only add to her confusion where her dad was concerned.

He opened the door to the kitchen to find her sitting at the island waiting for him. It was clear from the look on her face, she knew something was up.

"I need to tell you some things that have been happening since your dad died."

Her guard went up right away. He could see it in her face, in the way she tensed her shoulders.

"Okay."

"Your dad's apartment was broken into shortly after he died. The only thing missing was his medicine."

"Why is that a big deal?"

"Well, it might not be. It's just that the doctor that was treating him seems a little fishy. He got real squirrelly when a friend of a friend on the police force went to talk to him—"

"Wait." She held up her hand. "You had the police go see his doctor? What for?"

"Mostly because I just felt like something was off. I just wanted to know why someone would break in and only take medicine."

Her jaw was tense as she replied. "So, what did the police think?"

He hesitated. He didn't want to give her the police's theory, but he had no choice now. "That your dad might have been selling his meds and that whoever he was selling them to broke in to get the last of the stash. I think they're wrong."

She raised a brow and he continued. "I went down to the clinic thinking I might talk to your dad's doctor myself. I ended up talking to a woman named Darla. Your dad had introduced me to her a few times. She told me her friend or her husband—I'm not really sure what their relationship was, but Jimmy, that's his name. Anyway, he had also died of a heart attack. She gave me an empty pill bottle and said he'd been given some medicine by the doctor but he died anyway. She wasn't really clear, but things just don't seem right. She made it sound like he'd gotten the meds as part of a drug trial."

"I don't understand, Jax. What are you saying?"

He took a deep breath and plowed on. No sense stopping now. "I don't think your dad's death was an accident."

"Are you kidding me?" She stood now and he could see the confusion and disbelief in her eyes. He could also see her walls going up. He didn't blame her. It was the first time he'd said what he'd been thinking out loud and he was shocked to hear it, even though it had been brewing in his mind for some time.

She turned away from him looking out the window.

Shit. He knew this was a bad idea. "I'm sorry, Mia. I didn't mean to upset you. I just felt like you should know what was going on."

She turned to him with hurt eyes. "I just—for once, I want things to be simple where my dad is concerned. Just for once." She closed her eyes and turned away again and Jax waited, not sure what else to say.

He walked to her, circling his arms around her and pulling her back to lean against him.

"I'm sorry." He didn't know how to express what he was thinking to her. He wished things could be easy with her dad, too. That Leo had somehow never left or had gotten his shit together in time to go back to his daughter and wife. To have a relationship with them.

Then again, if Leo had done that, he and Jax wouldn't have met and maybe he and Mia wouldn't be standing here together. The thought was a selfish one, but he couldn't deny the feeling once it hit. He wanted her in his life.

She didn't turn back to face him when she spoke. "Is that why you took me out to dinner, Jax? Do you need me to sign off on tests or ask the police to open an investigation? What do you need?"

"No. God no." The suggestion hit him in the gut. He couldn't believe she would think he'd had any kind of motive in taking her out. He turned her to face him and kept his arms around her, not wanting to break the connection. "I took you to dinner because I like you and I want to be with you, to get to know more of you. I can't stop thinking about you when I'm not with you. Can't keep my hands off you when I am."

She studied his face as if looking for answers. He waited, letting out a breath when she gave a small nod.

"What now?"

He didn't know if she was asking about her dad's case or about things between them so he went with her dad's case.

"A detective with the New Haven PD is looking into it. He's a friend of someone I work with. A good guy. He'll call as soon as he hears anything."

She frowned. "I feel like we should do something. I don't think I want to just wait and see."

She looked up at him and he knew just what she was feeling. He wasn't really happy about just sitting and waiting for Jarrod to do his thing, either.

"Maybe we can go talk to Darla, see if she knows who the other people are who died. We can try to talk to people they knew. I doubt these guys will talk to Jarrod, but they know me. They might talk to me."

She didn't answer. Just grabbed her purse and keys and headed for the door. He was right behind her.

CHAPTER 21

JAX WAS quiet as he drove around the streets of New Haven adjacent to the homeless shelter. They'd filled the drive from Hartford with easy talk, and Mia had been relieved that things hadn't been awkward between them after falling asleep on the couch together the night before. For having spent the night on the couch, she felt remarkably good.

She studied Jax's profile as he looked intently through the glass of the windshield. Everything about him was intense and focused, and she wondered if this was what he'd been like when he was a Corpsman overseas. She knew he could laugh and have fun just as easily, though, and she liked seeing both sides of him. It was an appealing combination that had her fascinated.

"There she is," Jax said, nodding toward a small group of people sitting on a concrete ledge near the train tracks. He pulled past the group to an open parking spot on the next block and turned to Mia. "Ready?"

"You bet," she said and pulled the door handle, taking a

deep breath. It seemed surreal. What on earth were they doing investigating her father's death?

Before she could think much of it, Jax had joined her, putting one hand on her back and steering her toward the group. She could feel the eyes of Darla and the three men with her turn toward her and Jax, but within seconds, the faces broke out in smiles of recognition.

There were murmured greetings before Jax introduced her. "This is Mia, Leo Kent's daughter." The words sounded strange to her ears, and a pang of wistfulness hit her. She was startled by it. She'd longed to have her father in her life as a child, but she'd largely given up that dream as an adult. The introduction reminded her of the abandoned hope. "Mia, this is Darla, Moses, DJ, and Acorn."

"Leo was a good man," Moses said, and Darla nodded. DJ and Acorn wandered away as Moses continued. Jax couldn't remember ever hearing the two men talk. "Saved my sweet ass once."

He laughed, a harsh loud laugh. "Sorry, miss. My language ain't fit for mixed company, but that's the truth of it. Fucking hoodlums beating my ass bad in an alley. I'd just curled up in a ball ready to take it and hope like hell I came out alive, but Leo came and chased 'em off. Picked up a big freaking pipe from a dumpster and ran 'em off."

Before Mia could say anything, Moses walked away, repeating, "Good man. He was a good man."

Jax grinned and turned to Darla, and Mia was thankful for the reprieve. She hadn't thought about the fact that some of the people they would meet would know her father and have stories for her.

"Darla, we wanted to ask you a little more about Jimmy's death. Would that be okay?"

Mia liked how gentle he was with the woman's feelings. It didn't surprise her at all, though.

Darla's face clouded but she nodded and sat back down on the concrete wall. Jax sat next to her with Mia on his other side.

"I spoke to someone in the New Haven Police Department," Jax began. Mia wondered if the homeless people in New Haven had a good or bad relationship with the police. From what she'd seen in the newspaper, New Haven was pretty innovative in its community policing approach. She couldn't remember all the details, but she knew every officer who graduated from the academy in New Haven spent a minimum of a year on a walking patrol route.

When Darla didn't comment, Jax continued. "The detective I spoke with found that a number of other men who went to the clinic have died from heart attacks this month. He and his partner are going to look into things, but I thought I'd see what we could find out. Do you mind if I ask if you were married to Jimmy?

There seemed to be apology in Jax's voice, as though he knew it was offensive to pry into this woman's life.

The color drained from Darla's face as she shook her head, and her voice shook when she answered this time. "No. We never saw any need to make it official, not to mention paying for the license wasn't really in our budget." She snorted out a laugh, but there was bitterness behind it as she gazed around at where she and Jimmy had made a home of sorts. Mia wondered what circumstances had brought the woman to the streets in the first place and then what had kept her there. Why hadn't she and Jimmy been able to climb their way out?

She supposed there were any number of reasons things could get so bad it became impossible to turn their lives around. Maybe mental health issues, or some physical disability that made work impossible. It had to be hard to go for job interviews or show up at a job every day when you didn't have clean clothes or a shower, never mind transportation to get to work.

Maybe they'd just gotten in so far over their heads, they couldn't see a way out? Just thinking about it made Mia's heart ache for her father. She knew alcohol had played a large part in his being on the streets, but thinking of the years he spent living without before Jax came and helped him get his head above water killed her.

"Do you know anything about the other deaths?" Jax's question pulled Mia back to the present and she focused on Darla's answer.

"Sure," Darla said nodding. "There were Big Sam and Ray Ray. Don't know about the others."

"Do you know if they were seeing one of the clinic doctors?"

Darla frowned. "I don't know. Could be. I didn't like Big Sam at all. He had a mean streak and drank too damned much. Me and Jimmy stayed as far away from him as we could." Her eyes teared a little as she talked about Jimmy and Mia could see the pain marring the woman's face. It was true heartache. "I didn't know Ray Ray very well, either. He was new around here. Came up from Texas or Florida, I think."

"Is there anyone we could talk to who might know?" Jax pressed.

Darla grinned at him, but shook her head. "No. But there are people *I* can talk to who might know."

Jax laughed. "All right." He handed her a card. "My cell number is on there. Call me anytime you hear something."

Before they could stand, Darla turned intense eyes on

Mia. "He really was a good man. Helped a lot of us, and never asked for anything from anyone in return."

It took Mia a minute to process that Darla was talking about her dad. She didn't know what to say, but Darla didn't seem to care whether she answered or not.

"When this guy first started showing up and bringing your dad food or cash" she said, nodding her head in Jax's direction, "your dad never kept that all for himself. He always knew which of us was most in need. The food or cash got doled out to those who needed it."

"I never knew for sure, but I suspected," Jax said.

"Thank you," Mia finally said, realizing she was thankful to Darla for sharing the little bit of information about her dad. As confused as she was about him, she couldn't help wanting to know more about him. And she was starting to see that maybe he'd left and stayed away all of these years because he truly did believe she and her mother were better off for it.

Darla nodded and smiled, then seemed to think of something else and added, "He was proud of you, too."

"What?" *Proud of me?* She'd only found him recently and they hadn't even talked about who she was or what she did or anything.

"Yep. When you graduated from high school, from college. Proud days. He told everyone."

Mia looked to Jax and shook her head, before turning back to Darla. "But how could he know?"

"He took the bus up to Hartford both times. Watched you from a distance. He'd always be hurting for days afterward, real quiet and withdrawn, but eventually he'd tell us how proud he was of you."

"You knew him for that long?" Jax asked and Darla nodded.

"Mm hmm, long time. We met Leo in New Orleans. We all came up here together."

"But I don't understand," Mia said. "How could he know when I was graduating or where I went to college?"

Darla shrugged. "Kept track somehow."

The woman seemed to think the conversation had gone on long enough, because she got up and walked away, leaving Mia staring open mouthed at Jax.

"He loved you," he said softly.

Mia was beginning to believe it.

"Darla!" she called out and waited for the woman to turn back. "Thank you."

It wasn't enough. Not nearly enough. But Darla nodded and smiled as if to say she understood, and Mia had a feeling she did.

CHAPTER 22

MIA FELT nerves stirring in her stomach as she and Jax walked to her front door. He'd driven up to Hartford two days after they'd fallen asleep on the couch together to take her to dinner.

She wanted to ask him to come inside but didn't know if he'd want to.

Of course he wants to. What man doesn't?

The only problem was, she didn't want him to come in just because it was an offer of sex and no man would turn free sex down. She really liked him. And she wanted him to want her back. To like her just as much.

He pulled her into his arms at the door and lowered his mouth to hers, beginning with a kiss that made her head spin. His mouth felt so right on hers. Strong but soft at the same time. Controlling but not in a way that made her want to run screaming for the hills. In a way that made her toes curl and her heart race.

She ran her hands over the muscles in his arms, up to his shoulders, and around his neck. She liked the way his hair felt, all clipped short and military when she ran her fingers over it. It tickled her fingers, but not in a funny tickle kind of way. It tantalized and aroused.

"Mia," he groaned, and she pressed her hips against his.

"This is about to get R-rated on my porch," she whispered.

"Then get us inside."

She turned and fumbled in her purse for keys as he pressed against her backside and ran his hands around her waist. She whimpered as she turned the key in the lock and let them inside.

She dropped her purse on the floor as Jax slid the lock into place behind them.

"Hold on," he said, not giving her a minute to process what he said as he scooped her into his arms.

"Yes, sir." She didn't know what possessed her to say those two words, but his eyes heated with a mixture of amusement and desire as he walked toward the back of her house.

She ran her mouth along his neck, loving the growl that came from him in response.

"Which way, Mia?"

"Last room. Right." She went back to his neck, only pausing when he laid her on the bed.

He came down on top of her. "My turn."

She was somewhat lost after that, as his mouth did things to her that she hadn't ever experienced. He licked and nipped at her skin until she thought she might explode. He'd stripped her of her clothes before removing his own.

He was nothing short of perfection. Every muscle taut and sculpted, as if he were made from clay. She ran her hands over his body, not wanting the connection between them to end.

"God, you're beautiful, Mia. So soft."

"I was just thinking the same thing about you. Except not the soft part." She laughed, but he stole her laughter and her breath when his mouth caught her breast. She moaned and pressed her body closer.

He rolled her then, pulling her on top of him, but she felt him still, then curse. He pushed her to the side and sat, pulling the sheet off from around his prosthesis. He sat with his back to her on the side of the bed.

"Jax?" She pulled the sheet over herself, wondering if he was having second thoughts or if she'd said or done something wrong.

He looked over his shoulder at her and she realized he looked tense and nervous. Maybe this wasn't about her after all.

"What is it, Jax?" She reached her hand out toward him and touched his shoulder, surprised to see him glance away.

"Will it freak you out if I take my leg off?"

"No." She shook her head. "Why would that freak me out?" She sat up, drawing the sheet over her. She'd never seen him act at all worried about his leg around her, but it occurred to her she'd never seen him without his prosthesis.

"I just—" He looked almost apologetic and ran a hand through his hair. "I just haven't done this—" He cut off again then met her eyes and seemed to brace himself for a blow. "I just haven't been with anyone since I lost my leg."

That took her more than a minute to process. "Wait. You haven't been with a woman at all since then?"

"No." He shook his head, his mouth a grim line.

She looked at him but he still wasn't looking her way.

"Knock it off."

His brows went up and his eyes met hers now. "Knock what off?"

"The ... the ..." she sputtered and waved her hand in his

direction. "Whatever *this* is. The pity party or whatever. I don't care about your leg and I don't care that you have to take care of yourself and your needs sometimes. You're allowed."

He watched her for a minute before a smile broke over his face. He leaned in and kissed her, softly, firmly. This was a different kiss. Where the ones before had been about heat and need, this was all emotion and heart. It was connection on a different level and it stopped her heart.

He broke the kiss and looked at her, still holding her face in his hands, then turned and removed his prosthesis. He set it between the bed and the nightstand, pulled off the layers of material she'd seen between the prosthesis and his limb and turned them inside out before laying them next to the leg.

He moved with ease back over her, causing her to lay back as his body came down over her. Confident Jax was back and she sighed and slipped closer to him. He lost no time, his mouth and hands finding those spots that sent her into a frenzy so easily, she forgot to worry about his leg or any questions about how he was feeling. She was lost as he took control.

Jax produced a condom from somewhere and covered himself, his eyes locked on hers.

She wrapped her legs around his waist as he settled himself above her. She whispered his name as he entered her, slowly stretching her. Every nerve in her body felt like it was being stroked by him. It was both the most pleasure she'd ever felt and not enough at the same time.

She wrapped her arms around his shoulders and pulled him down to kiss her as he found a rhythm that had her pressing her hips up to meet him stroke for stroke.

He rolled them, pulling her up on top of him and

holding her hips as she ground down on him in sheer heaven. She came almost instantly, and watched as he ground his teeth, orgasm taking over as his body tensed beneath her.

She collapsed in a heap on top of him. "I feel like Jell-O," she said as he ran his hand up and down her spine. "Like very happy, sated Jell-O."

He laughed and grazed his mouth over her temple, loving the feel of her, the sound of their heavy breathing filling the room.

Moments later, she lifted herself off him and he rolled to the side, taking care of the condom. When he pulled her back into his arms, pressing her against the full length of his body, she couldn't help thinking how well they fit together. It was a foolish school girl thought, but it was the last thing in her mind as they drifted to sleep.

Jax walked through the hallways of the New Haven Shelter. He'd been hoping to see the director, but he was out. The woman out front had sent him back to see the deputy director.

The name plate on the outside of her office read *Carissa Hastings*. The door was shut but he could hear voices. She was on the phone and she was using the speaker function, letting Jax listen in.

"Yes, we'll pledge seventy-five thousand for this year's gala. That's no problem, Carrie," said the voice on speaker phone. Jax couldn't help but listen. Who had that kind of money?

No one in his world. Actually, that wasn't true, he realized with a jolt. His bosses at Sutton Capital could, and he was friends with them, but he tended to forget they had that kind of money. He sure as hell didn't. Not that he was poor. Far from it, but who writes a check for seventy-five grand like it was nothing.

"Thank you so much, Warrick. I knew I could count on Simms."

"Are you going ahead with the expansion of the clinic?"

"Well, I was actually hoping to talk to you about that. We want to use some of the space that's been freed up in the shelter as new clinic space and expand our services."

"Is there a problem with the plan?"

"I've heard rumors that Branson Medical might pull their funding of the medical clinic. That would be a huge blow. I don't think we'd make the expansion work if we lost them."

Jax began to make mental notes of the names he was hearing.

The woman's voice continued, as Jax moved closer to the door. "Do you think you could talk to Meredith Ball at the gala? Maybe help her see how important it is to continue to fund the clinic?"

"You got it," said the man on the phone. "I think Meredith Ball is friends with Jonathan. Maybe I can drag him out of the lab and get him to the Gala."

Carrie laughed. "I'll believe it when I see it."

The man laughed along with her. "Well, either way, I'll see what I can do."

"Thank you, Warrick."

"Anytime. Talk to you soon, Carrie."

The room went quiet and Jax knocked on the door.

"Come in."

He opened the door to find a tall blonde woman rising from behind her desk. She looked surprised to see a stranger at her door and he wondered if the woman at the front desk was supposed to send him back here or not.

"Hi, Ms. Hastings. I'm Jax Cutter."

She recovered quickly and he couldn't help thinking she seemed completely out of place in the shelter. She had the regal bearing of someone raised among wealth and privilege. He wondered briefly what had her slumming down at the shelter.

"How can I help you, Mr. Cutter?" She offered her hand and he shook it. *Yes. Soft hands.* Those were the hands of a pampered woman. Her outfit matched. She wore tailored pants and a blouse he'd bet cost a month of his salary and seemed completely out of place in the shelter.

"I'm a friend of Leo Kent's."

Her face softened. "I was sorry to hear about Leo's death."

"You knew Leo?" Jax asked. He knew Leo spent time at the shelter but he was surprised the woman before him would know any of the shelter residents by name.

"Yes," she smiled. "He was a kind man."

What she said was true, but Leo was also a private man. Jax realized he didn't know what he was hoping to find out from her. He'd come here just hoping to get a sense about the shelter. To poke around a little and ask some questions. He focused on the conversation he'd just overheard.

Jax was winging it and way out of his element. "I was thinking of making a donation to the shelter in Leo's name."

"That's very generous of you."

"Uh, so I saw something about an annual gala you hold each year to raise money for the clinic?"

She nodded and smiled. "Yes. It's one of our biggest fundraisers of the year."

"So, it's what? A giant party?"

"Something like that," she said. Her phone began to ring and she glanced at it, but didn't interrupt their conversation. "It's a ball of sorts. Black tie. Our largest donors come out for it each year."

He'd heard the names Simms and Warrick. Jax knew he'd heard those names before. And some medical company. Branson Medical. He wondered if that could be the company giving out medicine at the clinic.

"Wouldn't you save money if you just asked them for donations instead of putting on a ball?"

She laughed as the phone stopped ringing, likely rolling over to voicemail. "I'm afraid that's just not how these thing work. I'd love it if my donors would just whip out the check book. Sadly, they have to be wined and dined. It's a publicity thing for them. A chance to be seen supporting the clinic, to have their names appear in the news in a positive light."

Jax wondered if she knew about the deaths that seemed to be plaguing the shelter and the clinic.

"It seems several other homeless people have died recently either at the shelter or the clinic in the last few months. All of them from heart attacks. That seems unusual."

She looked like he'd struck her, and if he wasn't mistaken, he thought he saw real sorrow there. Carrie Hastings might not seem like she belonged in this environment, but she sure as hell seemed to care about the work they did here. "I'm sorry. What?"

"You weren't aware?"

"Yes. I am, but it's not something I'm going to discuss with you, Mr. Cutter." Her walls had gone up and he knew he wouldn't get anything more out of her.

The phone began to ring again and she glanced at it,

then back to him. "I'm sorry, Mr. Cutter. I've really got to take this. The gala is only a few weeks away and I've got a million things to do. Would you like me to get you some material on donations for the gala?"

"That's all right," he said. "I can see you're busy. I'll come back another time."

She nodded and picked up the phone, answering before he'd even walked away.

After texting Jarrod the names Branson Medical, Warrick, Jonathan, and Simms to look into, Jax found himself on the road to Hartford without any conscious thought. All he knew as he drove was that he wanted to see Mia again. He'd felt more connected to her than he had to any woman. He liked being with her, and it wasn't just about the sex. He liked her as a person. He wanted to talk with her as much as he wanted her in his bed.

She made him feel good, happier than he'd been in a long time. He hadn't realized, until now, how empty his life had been. He had good friends, a job he loved, but with her, everything seemed better. Like the lights had been turned on or something. He shook his head at how stupid and corny his thoughts were at the moment, then grinned when he realized he didn't care.

He pulled up to her house and was relieved to see her car in the driveway. He waited after knocking and realized he was damned near holding his breath.

Confusion crossed her face for a brief moment before that mouth he loved to kiss broke into a wide smile.

"Surprise," he said, stepping through the door and into her arms.

"You're crazy," she said laughing as she wrapped her arms around him. "You'll be exhausted from all this driving back and forth if you keep coming up here on weeknights."

"True," he agreed before catching her mouth in a kiss and putting an end to their conversation. He was going to be very tired in the morning, but he had a feeling it would only get worse. He couldn't go through the week without seeing her. Without holding her, making love to her. And if that meant he was worn out for meetings at work and had to walk around like a zombie most days, he was good with that.

* * *

Mia's heart raced as Jax rested his head on her stomach, one arm running lazy trails over her hip.

She knew now why she had been with Nick. She could see it so clearly, it almost made her laugh at how obvious it was. Nick had been safe. She never would have felt anything powerful and overwhelming for him. It was why she'd also not felt anything when she'd decided it was over.

If Nick had walked away from her at any point, her feelings and her pride would have been hurt. That would have been the extent of it, though. She'd have been bruised, but not broken.

With Jax, the strength of her feelings frightened her. Because if he left, if it ended between them, she knew she'd be crushed.

Even knowing why her dad had left her and her mom hadn't quieted the doubts that were tearing through her. She'd thought maybe knowing the truth would make it better, but it simply hadn't.

All the times she'd heard her mother crying alone in her bedroom when she thought Mia had gone to bed echoed in her mind. She'd thought she would never let herself be that way with a man. She wouldn't let her feelings grow so powerful they could take over like that and make her weak.

But she had. She was halfway there with Jax. Oh, who was she kidding? There was no halfway about it. She was there. And it terrified her.

She traced a long jagged scar on the inside of his thigh with one finger. The raised skin was smooth, in a way that belied the violence done to his body.

"Close call," she said, as she reached its end, a mere few inches from his groin.

He laughed, and she smiled back at him, but her heart was pounding. She had a feeling that had been a *very* close call and she was no longer talking about the loss of anatomy he might have suffered. She couldn't imagine what it had been like to serve in the war the way he had, and to come that close to death.

Jax lifted up on an elbow and stared into her eyes, making her want to look away.

"You're thinking too much. I can feel it." He stated it as a simple fact, but there was questioning in his eyes.

"I'm sorry. I don't think I can help it." Mia didn't know what to say. Wasn't she the one who should be wanting to talk about her feelings? Shouldn't the guy be the one to avoid talks like this?

He raised his brows and kept his focus on her, waiting her out.

She let out a slow breath and ran a hand over his chest, avoiding his eyes. "I just didn't want to feel this way with anyone. I told myself I'd avoid it."

She could almost feel him freeze in place, but he covered it well. "Feel what way?" he asked quietly.

"Out of control. Overwhelmed." She sought for the right words to tell him what she was feeling.

He ran a warm, solid hand over her arm and brushed a kiss to her lips. "What else are you feeling?"

His voice was soft, low and somehow held a quality that soothed her. Steadied her. She took a breath. "Excited." A pause, then, "happy."

"And scared?" he asked, reading her mind.

She nodded. "And scared."

He put a hand on her cheek and turned her face to his, the caress of his thumb on her cheek firm and strong. "I want this with you, Mia. Not the sex." He smiled and she blushed. "As amazing as making love to you is, that's not what I'm talking about. I want *us*. I want to be with you, to find out everything there is to know about you. To build on this."

She raised her arms up and kissed him, needing to end the talk. It was becoming all too real for her, and she knew he couldn't make any promises. They were only just beginning this relationship. It's not like she expected him to declare his love and promise to never leave her. She didn't expect that.

She just hated the feeling of knowing she was putting herself on the line with this. Of knowing she was making herself vulnerable to him. Because that's what she was now. Vulnerable and spread open.

She let his kiss take over, let the feelings of his hands and mouth on her make all of the worry and unease fade to the background. He found his way to her breasts, grazing one nipple with his teeth, then suckling as it beaded beneath his tongue, before moving to the other. The sensation shot straight through her, bringing all of her nerve endings to sizzling attention.

She spread her legs as he rolled to settle himself between them and she clung to his shoulders while his mouth continued to torment and tease. This. She would focus only on this and force her frantic mind to shut down.

To stop the panic. Because being with this man might be frightening, but it was also the most incredible feeling she'd ever experienced. And for once, she was going to allow herself to experience it fully and not focus on what might come down the road.

CHAPTER 23

MIA TRIED to keep herself from walking around with a dopey smile on her face, but she had a feeling she wasn't succeeding. Her assistant had asked her a few times that day why she looked like she had a secret she wasn't sharing.

She walked down the stairs of the three story building that housed the law firm and let the smile spread across her face. No one could see it now, so she might as well enjoy it. Jax had spent the night, leaving early in the morning to drive to New Haven. He'd said the commute was worth it.

Again, she grinned. "This is getting ridiculous," she said aloud. She wondered briefly if anyone could die of an overdose of *happy*.

She saw the flash of movement in the shadow behind her as she rounded the staircase to the second story. It wasn't in time to do anything about it. She was hit in the side of the head and pain reeled through her. She fell to the floor, a large body pressing down over her, pinning her to the ground.

"Close your eyes." The voice was terrifying and cruel and fear like she'd never known pressed down on her chest, making it all but impossible to breathe. Why hadn't she had her mace in her hand?

She didn't have time to think. She shut her eyes, part in response to the directive as the man pressed down on her, pain ramping up, and part in response to the bright light that shone in her eyes. She couldn't move.

"I just need a little video for your boyfriend." He laughed like he'd said something funny. "It's too bad we don't have more time together. We could have fun."

The man ran his tongue up her face and Mia sank back away from it, trying to press herself into the ground. Trying to move away from the grotesque gesture.

He shook her a little and she pressed her eyes closed even further. She had the sudden thought that maybe if he knew she couldn't identify him, he'd let her live. "Now, say something for your boyfriend."

She let out a sob through clenched teeth. He shook her again, her head cracking on the pavement beneath her. "Say something for the camera bitch."

"Please," she gasped as pain and fear battled for control.

"Not your best performance, but it'll have to do," he said, almost cheerily.

A door slammed above them and the sound of footsteps came from the stairs above.

The light suddenly disappeared and the man fled, leaving Mia in a heap on the ground. She curled up in a ball, tears streaming down her face as she struggled to breathe.

"Mia! Jesus, Mia!"

She cried as arms wrapped around her. Familiar and safe.

* * *

"Ma'am?" Jarrod knocked on the door to the Medical Examiner's office and poked his head in.

Cal was looking into the names Jax had given him, trying to find out all he could about the shelter sponsors and the medical companies who might be connected to the clinic. If one of the large pharmaceutical companies was funding the clinic, maybe they'd managed to convince the clinic doctors to do some illegal drug testing in exchange for the influx of cash.

In the meantime, Jarrod had filled the medical examiner in by phone on their theory that someone was using the clinic to test a drug illegally, and asked her to pull the files she had for the deceased homeless people that had come up in their search.

"Hello, Detective Harmon." The dark haired woman in her fifties waved him in. Jarrod was always surprised when the ME remembered him. Dr. Kane apparently remembered everyone's name and even remembered details about people's kids and pets. Jarrod didn't have either.

"Thank you for seeing me."

She nodded, then picked up a stack of files, leafing through them as she spoke. "I pulled the files for all of the deaths of persons without permanent housing in heart-related incidents in the last three months. Three were claimed by a family member in another state. The others went unclaimed."

"So you have the bodies?" He said and then realized he sounded a little too excited about that. She frowned at him.

"No. Unfortunately, those cases were more than thirty days ago." At his blank look, she expanded: "They were cremated after thirty days according to law."

"What happens to the ashes?" He was no longer asking because of the case. He felt the need to know if these people had been given any kind of service. To know what happened to their remains when they weren't claimed by family.

She smiled but it was a tight, sad smile. "They're scattered in the city memorial garden. Myself and a minister from one of the local churches always attend and say a few words. Sometimes there are a few other people from our church who attend. Volunteers."

Jarrod didn't know what to say. It had never before occurred to him to think about what happened to the men and women he saw on the streets when they passed. In some ways, as a cop, you had to tune those things out or you'd lose your mind.

She gave him the kind of look that said she knew this was dawning on him for the first time. "This was a life, just like your life and my life. Somewhere, someone once shared a life with this person, loved them. My friends and I believe someone should be there to memorialize their death. It's a small thing, but it's something we committed to a long time ago, and it's a practice we've maintained."

She said the words very matter-of-factly, but he could see there was a lot of feeling behind them.

Jarrod nodded. They both seemed to take a moment before she dragged them back on course. "So," she said, picking up the folders again, "the remains of the unclaimed gentlemen have already been scattered. Because their cases crossed my desk, I do have blood and tissue samples on file, but I would need a court order to run any tests on those. There aren't any tissue samples on file for Leo Kent."

Jarrod nodded. "His case never came through your office, right?"

"That's correct. He was under the care of a doctor who signed his death certificate, so his body was cremated without any tissue or blood collection. I think your best course of action is to contact the next-of-kin for one of those who were claimed. I've got tissue and blood samples on file, but I'll need next-of-kin to sign off on the tests."

She handed him the folders. "The forms they'll need to sign are on top."

Jarrod stood. "Thank you, doctor."

"Oh and one more thing. If there is a pre-market drug involved, it will take some time to track down what it is. You need to be prepared for that."

"Wouldn't the FDA have that on file?" Jarrod asked, brows coming together.

"Uh huh." She nodded her head. "But getting that info involves us jumping through some hoops. There are trade secrets and things that have to be protected. The FDA will give law enforcement access to the info, but we've got to sign non-disclosure agreements and things first. Just know it's not going to be an immediate result. It takes time for us to make it happen."

"Thank you." He had to bite back a sigh. It never was easy, was it?

She nodded as if answering his unspoken question, then turned back to her desk, already moving on to her next project. He had a feeling her work was a lot like his. It never ended.

CHAPTER 24

JARROD FINISHED a call with Jax and looked to his partner. "We ready?"

"Yeah," Cal walked down the hall toward the deputy director's office as he gestured toward Jarrod's phone. "Who was that?"

"Jax. He's just finishing up work for the day and wanted to see if we had anything new. He was able to talk to Darla the other day, and she said she and Jimmy were never married. She said she'd ask around about the other men who suffered heart attacks recently, but she just called him and she hasn't been able to find anything out."

"Damn, so if she and Jimmy weren't married, she can't give us permission to run any tests on the blood and tissue samples."

"Nope. We either need to find the next-of-kin for one of the others, or get a court order to perform the testing." Jarrod rubbed his forehead. He felt the start of a headache coming on and made a mental note to get some caffeine into his system one way or another as soon as they finished up here.

"We don't have enough for that."

Cal wasn't saying anything Jarrod hadn't been thinking. He gestured down the hall. "Let's see what Carrisa Hastings has to tell us."

They knocked on the deputy director's door and a tall blonde woman opened the door.

"What can I do for you, Detectives?" Carrisa Hastings asked after introductions were made and identification had been produced. She offered a polite smile and he immediately wished for a warmer one. The kind you'd give someone you were genuinely happy to see, not a cop.

He frowned to himself at the odd thought. He often noticed people's reactions to the badge, but he never wished for a warmer reception while on the job. The people they interviewed were simply people he needed information from. Nothing more.

"We're just doing some follow up on the death of Leo Kent," Cal said smoothly. Jarrod was happy to let Cal take the lead on this one as he watched the woman in front of him intently. If he'd hoped to see any kind of reaction to Leo Kent's name, he would have been disappointed. She kept her mask in place.

"I'm not sure what I can tell you, but go ahead and ask."

The men stepped further into the room. "Do you know if Leo Kent was taking part in any drug trials?"

They'd decided to begin with asking about Leo Kent, then see what happened when they brought the other men's names into the conversation.

She sighed. "I'm afraid drug trials are all too popular around the shelter."

"And you're not fond of them." Jarrod said. It was a statement not a question. He'd seen it in her face as soon as Cal asked the question.

"Not at all." She shook her head and waved a hand at the two empty chairs in front of her desk. "Drug trials can seem like a panacea to the homeless. Some are outpatient but they're paid for participation. Others have the added bonus of being in-patient, in which case, they get a roof over their head for a time, meals and snacks, and video games all day long."

"Tempting for someone who has very little, if any prospects." Jarrod had never thought about it before, but it made perfect sense. Many drug trials needed people who didn't have the targeted illness at first, just to test how the drug was handled by the human body, if it had any side effects, that kind of thing.

"That's not the worst of it. We've learned over time that homeless people will even go so far as to begin using heroin or other drugs to get into a heroin cessation trial, for example." Now she seemed to be thawing a bit. She seemed to genuinely care about the medical testing that was being done on the population she served.

"Wow. The trial organizers can't pick up on that somehow?" Jarrod frowned as he thought through the implications of that for all involved. For the person who was risking building a real habit that wouldn't be helped by the trial. For the trial organizers and physicians whose results could very well be skewed by their participation. It was an all-around bad idea.

She raised her hands, palms to the sky. "How could they? The person comes in and tests positive for heroin in their system. They fake the right history. Heaven knows they've seen what the addiction looks like in their time on the streets. They know the language, the signs. They can fake it well enough to get into the trial."

She leaned toward the men a fraction. "Things are a little better now. Have you heard of Zero: 2016?"

"Pretend we haven't," Jarrod said. He had but his knowledge of the program was vague. He wanted details from someone who knew more about it than he did.

She nodded. "It's an initiative that began with homeless veterans, but we're expanding it now to the entire homeless population. It's a national program to make homelessness rare, brief, and non-recurring. Connecticut was one of only four states to sign on—the rest are cities or municipalities. We're now poised to be the first state to end chronic homelessness and reach the goal of functional zero for our homeless population."

"What does that mean?" Cal asked. "Functional zero? I mean, I've seen a huge decrease in the homeless around here lately, but it seems to me they're still out there."

Jarrod was hesitant to agree with Cal, given the woman's clear commitment to the goal, but Cal was right. They'd just walked by several people who looked like they were living on the streets on the way inside.

She nodded. "It's a technical definition. It doesn't mean that homelessness doesn't exist. It means that we're at such low numbers that we're able to identify people either before they lose their housing, or immediately afterward, and are able to get them into permanent housing within thirty days. It also includes anyone who refuses assistance in getting off the streets."

She didn't have to explain that one to Cal or Jarrod. They both knew that sometimes, people refused help.

"And Connecticut has done this with veterans?" Jarrod asked.

"Yes. And we're close on all others. It's meant a big shift in how our organization functions. We've freed up some of the space we were using for temporary housing before. We'll be making that into additional clinic space to expand the medical services we can provide. If we get the funding we need," she added, with a smile that was much more natural now.

"Do you think that will put a stop to the drug trials?" Cal asked.

She shook her head slowly. "I don't think so. It might slow them down, but even after we find housing, there are always needs. Clothing, food, medical costs. They might not be as desperate, as driven, to get off the streets, but our people will always suffer from a level of need others aren't able to begin to understand."

Jarrod liked the way she called the people they helped "our people."

"So you don't know if Leo was taking part in any trials?" he asked.

"No I'm afraid I don't. We don't track them or have any involvement in them at all. They're independently run."

"So how do people find out about the tests?" The question came from Jarrod this time.

She pointed out toward the hallway. "They often post notices for the trials on our community boards. We allow it because it's one more way for us to get people in the door, where we can offer them services, try to help them. We've discussed stopping the practice, but honestly, it wouldn't stop the problem."

"And what about the clinic? Do they run any of the trials directly?" Jarrod asked.

She nodded. "Yes. But I'm afraid that's all I can tell you without a warrant. We sign a hefty confidentiality agreement every time we allow a trial to be run through the clinic."

"Is that standard?"

"Yes. It's reality." Her answer showed her pragmatic side. She seemed to care deeply for those she was trying to help, but he also had the sense that she was realistic about what she could and couldn't accomplish.

Jarrod wasn't surprised she'd clammed up at that. Honestly, she'd given them far more information than he'd thought she would, but all of the information had been pretty general. When it came to actually talking about the deaths or any specifics, she wasn't going to give them dick.

"If a person involved in one of the trials is sick enough to be admitted to a hospital or dies, does the company running the trial have some way to find out about that?" Jarrod wasn't really sure why he asked the question. Maybe part of him wanted to know if the people using these men even knew or cared that they'd died. If they were in fact even in a trial. They had yet to determine that for sure.

She shook her head. "No, there's no main registry or anything like that. I suppose if the person doesn't tell the hospital when they check in, then the company would only find out when the patient missed their appointments. They'd likely try to contact the person then, I suppose."

Jarrod and Cal glanced at one another and stood, silent communication easy after years partnering together. "Thank you for your time, Ms. Hastings," Cal said.

She smiled. "I'm sorry I don't have more answers for you. For what it's worth, I really liked Leo."

Jarrod nodded and the men walked out, neither one speaking. They had very little to go on other than gut instinct. If they didn't find anything concrete soon, they'd be forced to let this go and turn their attention to other cases. The thought ate at him. Jarrod hated to think they were letting down a segment of the population who couldn't speak for themselves.

"It's disgusting that drug companies can take advantage of people who have nothing like that," Jarrod said, opening the driver's side door of their unmarked sedan. "They dangle cash, a bed, food over their heads and give them God only knows what to put in their bodies. What choice do these people have but to grab at that?"

Cal shrugged. "It gets them off the streets for a bit, gets some food in their stomachs. Besides, the FDA doesn't let them run these tests until they're pretty damned sure they're safe, right? I mean, they have to."

Jarrod gave him a look that said he didn't buy that at all.

"Aw, come on," Cal said. "For the vast majority of these trials, they're just trying to find out if the meds are gonna give them the runs."

Jarrod shook his head. Sometimes, he didn't know if Cal was only arguing with him to mess with his head or what. He wasn't going to do this right now. "Yeah, but if we've got some doctor running around giving out meds in a trial that isn't FDA sanctioned, we've got bigger issues on our hands than ethics. We've got someone using our homeless population as Guinea pigs."

Cal's face grew dark, and there was no doubt in Jarrod's mind, they were on the same page on this one. "Yeah," Cal said. "But how do we prove that?"

Yeah. They needed to find something more than gut instinct, all right, because gut instinct wouldn't let them put a stop to this. It wouldn't help them put anyone away for the deaths of these men.

But damn, his gut was burning on this.

* * *

"Think of it as an insurance plan. For both of us." The man should have chosen someone of stronger character than Mark Coleman. The connection Coleman had to Simms Pharmaceutical was too damned good to pass up though, and with the history of heart attack in his family, he'd been an easy target.

The man had thought Coleman's gambling debt would be enough to keep Coleman under control, but he should have seen it for what it was. An indication of weakness. And that weakness was now causing trouble for him.

He had Leo Kent's friend and daughter sniffing all over the damned place and the police asking questions. It was what he wanted, eventually, but not now. Not when he didn't have everything in place yet.

He had paid muscle taking care of that little problem, but he needed to move up the timeline. There was a lot of groundwork to be laid.

Sykes nodded and took the fake paperwork. "I got it. I'll head over there after dark."

"You'll need this." He handed Sykes a keycard that wouldn't lead back to either of them. "Use the back entrance. The lobby and the front entrance have cameras, but they don't have cameras in any of the offices or clinic areas."

He watched as Sykes walked away. Now he needed to figure out an exit plan for Sykes as well. It never hurt to plan ten steps ahead of where you were. It was what he'd always practiced in the business world, and it was serving him well now. Plan ten steps out and with any luck you only had to make it to step three or four.

CHAPTER 25

JAX HEARD Chad behind him and turned. The man jogged to catch up and they walked through the doors to the garage together.

"Any plans tonight?" Chad asked.

"Probably gonna drive up to Hartford," he said, and the dumbass smile that he couldn't seem to stop crossed his face again.

Chad laughed. "You seemed a little tired during the meeting this afternoon. The drive getting to you?"

Before he could answer, his phone sounded a text alert. The next thirty seconds stopped his heart cold as rage and fear vied for control.

A video played on his phone. A man's hands pinning Mia to the ground. Her terrified face as she begged. Jax read the text beneath the video.

Back off if you don't want this pretty girl hurt.

He heard Chad curse beside him, but it was nothing compared to the string of curses that came from his own mouth. Jax's heart felt like it was trying to claw its way up his throat as he dialed Mia.

Please, God, please. He didn't ever remember praying this hard. Not even overseas, when demons from hell seemed to have been let loose on earth.

The phone rang several times before a man picked up.

"Hello."

"So help me, if you hurt her in any way, I'll rip your heart out of your chest and make your mother eat it for fucking breakfast, asshole."

Dead silence for a split second, then, "It's for you."

Jax heard shuffling and the muffled sounds of the phone moving, before Mia's voice came on the other end. "Jax? I'm okay."

His whole body seeming to deflate as relief flooded through him. "Where are you? Who's with you?"

"I was attacked in the stairwell at work. Nick found me." She started crying then, and he could tell she was struggling to talk.

Jax closed his eyes and sucked in air, and it struck him. That's what the world felt like when he thought of life without Mia. Like he couldn't breathe. Like there wasn't enough oxygen to sustain him.

He began to move to his Jeep. He needed to get to Mia.

"Oh hell, no. I'm driving." Chad put a large hand on Jax's shoulder and started steering him toward his truck. Jax didn't fight it. He rattled off the location of Mia's office to Chad, before opening the door to his truck.

"Mia?" Jax had a million other questions for her. *Are you okay? Are you scared? Did he hurt you?* He didn't ask any of them. His sole focus right now was on getting to her. "Can you hear me, honey? I'm on my way."

The man came back on the line then. "She's pretty shaken up, but physically, I think she's ok. She might need stitches on her forehead."

"Is this Nick?" Jax asked and was both grateful and resentful that the man was there to console Mia.

"Yeah." He paused. "I'll stay with her until you get here. The police are on their way."

"Thank you," Jax bit out.

As Chad pulled out into traffic, Jax talked to Mia. He talked to her until the police arrived and she had to hang up, saying stupid shit to make her laugh, to try to set her at ease.

CHAPTER 26

JAX DIDN'T KNOW when he'd get a full night's sleep again. He'd been awake the last few nights off and on watching Mia. He'd fall asleep for an hour or so, then wake with a start to see if she was still there. Still safe.

If he wasn't waking to check on her, she was waking from a nightmare. The whole right side of her face was discolored and swollen. She had a nasty bruise and sixteen stitches on her left temple where her attacker had struck her.

When she woke, he'd hold her hands so she didn't tear at the stitches in her panic. He'd calm her and whisper to her while she fell back to sleep. He wanted nothing more than to take that fear away from her. To make this go away for her.

Incredibly, she was doing better than he was during the day. It had been three days and he still wanted to lock her away and hide her somewhere safe. She was ready to take on the world. She jumped a little when they were out doing things, and she would start to look over her shoulder before she'd remind herself not to.

He could see her actively take a breath and force herself to move on whenever it happened. And it scared the crap out of him. Every morning, he'd drop her off at her office, then make the drive down to New Haven, showing up an hour late. He'd leave an hour early so he could get to Mia's office to pick her up. His bosses were understanding so far, but he wasn't sure how long he could keep it up.

Obsessive and possibly a little creepy?

Yeah. He was working on it.

Mia's eyes fluttered and she woke, thankfully, not with a jolt of panic this time.

"Morning," he said, leaning in to kiss her.

"Mmm." Her response came with a press of her body against his and her hand came up to press against his heart. He wondered if she knew just how much she touched him there.

He'd never tire of waking with her in his arms, even if he would someday need to give up on escorting her everywhere.

"So, I was thinking," she said.

"Yeah?" His brows rose.

"I think you should drive to New Haven from here today and I'll drive myself to work."

"Is that a gentle way of saying I need to back the hell off?"

She laughed. "Yes. And if that doesn't work, I'll tell you to back the hell off."

He laughed with her. Part of him loved that she wasn't letting the attack chase her into hiding. The other part, well, that was the caveman part. That guy was struggling.

He looked at her face and saw anxiety written in her features. Hell, was he doing that to her?

"What is it?" He asked.

"I need to tell you about something I didn't mention before."

She was trying to be casual, but Jax tensed. "Okay."

"I dated a guy in college," she began, and he saw clouds gather in her eyes. Oh man, he knew he was going to hate this story. "It was one of those relationships that started out hot and heavy right from the start."

Like ours. The thought hit Jax and he wondered just what had happened in this relationship in college. It sounded like the exact opposite of what she'd described with Nick. Maybe there'd been more to the way Mia was drawn to the comfortable safety of Nick.

"Yeah," he said.

"Then Gary got, well, a little too possessive. He was controlling and jealous all the time over absolutely nothing." She shivered as if a memory had washed over her and it wasn't a pleasant one. "It got really nasty, really scary, with him following me."

Jax had to focus on her face and steady his breathing. That, or hit a wall. The thought of someone doing that to her pissed him off. Except ... "Shit. And I'm acting that way now, aren't I?"

She smiled and shook her head. "No. I get where you're coming from. I feel the difference between you and Gary. Where he wanted to control and own me, you want to protect me. I get it. I'm frightened knowing the guy who attacked me is still out there, but I also won't live my life in fear because of that. I'll be careful, but not trapped by that knowledge. I need you to do that, too."

Jax kissed her softly. She was so damned strong. "What happened with Gary?"

"My mom and I confronted him, and said I'd get a restraining order. My mom told him she'd make damned sure the college knew about it. He was there on scholarship. It was enough to wake him up and get him to back off, thankfully."

"And now I'm triggering memories of this by being so overprotective. I'm sorry, Mia. I'm just—"

"An overbearing goon who's lucky I love him or ..." She seemed to freeze as her words came out. "I didn't ... that just ..."

Jax felt his heart thud to a halt and he studied her face. If someone had told him he'd hear those words and not panic a month ago, he'd have laughed. Now, he hoped like hell she wasn't about to take it back. "Do you mean it?"

She nodded, her answer a whisper. "Yes."

"Yes!" His echoing answer was anything but a whisper. He dropped his voice. "Yes."

The word kept coming from his mouth between kisses as he travelled the length of her body. He could hear her breathing grow irregular, and knew his touch was affecting her, but she tugged at his shoulders. He pushed himself up to look at her face again.

A slow grin started from deep within him and he didn't fight it. He loved this woman. Body, heart, and soul were hers for the taking. "I love you, Mia."

Her eyes went wide. "You do?"

He laughed again. That happened a lot around her. A hell of a lot, and it felt good.

Since she seemed to doubt the veracity of his claim, he set back to work, showing her just how much he loved her.

"If you really love me, you'll let me go," Mia said, hands on hips and eyes ablaze.

Well, damn. That one came back to bite him in the ass in a hurry. He rubbed a hand over his forehead.

"I will. I swear. I'm just going to need a minute to work up to it." He couldn't tell her that the words the man had said in the video played in his head again and again, never letting up.

I just need a little video for your boyfriend.

The police in Hartford were looking into the attack, but they hadn't found anything. The cameras in the stairwell had been broken before the attack. They knew the man was large. That was all the cameras showed as a masked man busted them up.

Jarrod had the police tech people looking into the video Jax had received but Jax already knew they wouldn't find squat there. He'd let Sam have his phone. Samantha might work at Sutton Capital and be married to one of Jax's friends, but she was also one of the most talented hackers in the country.

She'd traced the text back to a burner phone. Sam said it was unlikely the police would be able to find out anything more than that, and he believed her.

"Well, take a deep breath, and prep yourself, handsome. I gotta get to work." She looked pointedly down at his hand, clenching hers.

"Sorry." He kissed her softly and stepped back. "Have someone walk you to your car." Not an unreasonable request since whoever had done this was still out there.

"I will. Promise. And I'll see you in New Haven around seven."

"Okay." She stepped into her car and shut the door. "Text when you're on your way," he called through the window.

She laughed and rolled it down. "I'll call you and talk to you for the whole drive, if you want."

Good. That was good. Unless she was joking.

He watched her pull out and wondered if she had been joking. Hell, he'd call her either way.

CHAPTER 27

MIA FELT Jax squeeze her hand and looked over. That smile was something she knew she'd never get tired of seeing. The door opened and a tall man stood in the doorway. Beside him, a very pregnant—and nearly as tall—woman smiled at Mia and Jax.

After introductions, the woman reached out and pulled Mia in. "I'm so glad you guys could make it before the baby came. I've been dying to meet you."

"Me, too," Mia said and realized she really meant it. Jax had told her a lot about Sam and Logan, and she was only now realizing how much she'd kept people at arm's length much of her life. It was the same thing she did with Nick, and with the people she worked with. Never getting really close. Never truly letting them in.

Mia had a feeling it was because of her dad. If she didn't get close to people, it wouldn't hurt so much when they left.

Letting Jax into her life had been a risk for her, but it was one she found she was glad she'd taken. It was like some veil had been lifted and the world just looked brighter, *felt* brighter somehow. Richer.

Samantha led the group into a welcoming living room, and Mia and Jax watched as Logan helped her sit. Mia understood why Jax had said it was fun to tease the tough former SEAL. He looked like he wanted to dote and hover over his wife, but the glare she gave him had him moving back.

"So, I have to be blunt here," Sam said and Jax laughed.

"When are you not?"

"True." She gave him the kind of genuine smile that said they were used to ribbing one another. "But, listen, I've been craving pizza lately. Like, a *lot* of pizza. I ate it for breakfast this morning, but I'm craving it again. And I'm a crappy cook. So we ordered pizza. It should be here soon. Sorry we're not doing something more presentable, but that's just not me."

Mia felt an immediate connection to this woman who seemed to accept herself for who she was and assumed other people would too. Mia certainly would. She liked Sam.

The night continued from there in similar fashion with Mia grinning nearly nonstop at Sam's upfront manner and Jax's mostly successful attempts to get under Logan's skin.

They ate pizza and then had ice cream, because Sam insisted that's what "knocked up people" should eat. At one point, Sam pulled down the collar of her shirt and showed Mia moon shaped scars she had on the tops of her breasts. They were thin and faint.

"Trust me, they were a lot worse than that. I'll send you the name of the stuff I used to get them to fade. You'll want it for your forehead." She pointed to the spot on Mia's head where stitches nestled into the still-bruised landscape of her face.

Somehow, Samantha's comments didn't bother Mia.

She believed it was Sam's way of reaching out to help her, even if most people might not raise the issue of scarring with someone they barely knew.

The woman's directness was refreshing.

And then it was time for Logan's revenge on Jax.

The group stood near the front door to the condo saying their goodbyes when Sam doubled over, gripping her stomach. Pain creased her face and she cried out as Logan put his arms around her, taking her weight against him.

Mia froze, not sure what to do, but Jax sprang into action right away.

"Logan, move her to the couch and talk to her. Get her through this contraction, then we can see how far apart they are and call the doctor."

Mia stared at him. He was so calm. So in charge of everything. She knew Jax had jokingly told Logan he wouldn't be delivering Sam's baby in the living room, but when push came to shove, he was a rock. It was beyond sexy.

Of course, she supposed it was highly unlikely he'd actually be delivering this baby. If Sam was just having her first contraction, she'd have hours before she delivered. They had plenty of time to get to the hospital.

"Well, that was a let-down," Samantha said, standing suddenly, the pain gone from her face.

"Yeah, no kidding. When she did it to me, I damned near shit my pants. You're no fun." Logan looked at Jax like he'd stolen his puppy or something.

Mia turned to Jax to find him looking at her, the same shock she felt apparent on his face. She burst into laughter, only to be joined by him a second later as he shoved Logan on the shoulder.

"How many times did she do it to you before you stopped racing to get the car?" Jax asked Logan.

"Four." Logan's grin was big and Samantha looped her arms around his bicep and smiled at them. She was having entirely too much fun faking labor.

"You need to do that at the office Monday morning," Jax said over his shoulder as he and Mia headed out the door. "Right in front of Jack and Chad."

"You got it," Samantha called out behind them, a little too much glee in her voice.

CHAPTER 28

DARLA HEARD the last of the nurses leaving. The beeps of the alarm being set and the click of the lock in the door were the final indicators that the building was empty, save for her. She knew she had two hours before the cleaning staff came into the clinic.

The staff did a sweep of the building before locking up, but she'd been smart. She'd slipped into one of the bathrooms, then waited for them to move down the hall before hiding in one of the cabinets in the staff kitchen. No one would think to look in the cabinet with the coffee creamer and straws before closing up for the night.

Her heart pounded in her chest and her knees protested the cramped space, but she waited for several more minutes before climbing out. Jax and Mia had said they were talking to a detective about Jimmy's death, but she hadn't heard back from them in over a week.

It wasn't fair for Jimmy to be dead and no one be doing anything about it. It just wasn't right. She'd seen Max with one of those pill bottles, too, this morning. She'd tried to warn him, but he'd told her to mind her own business.

If the clinic and the cops didn't care that good people were dying, she'd do something about it. They were still giving out them pills. She wasn't going to let them do that. She might not have anything left in the world with Jimmy gone, but she had guts, and that was what she'd use to stop them. She'd get in there and find out what they were doing. There had to be evidence somewhere. This time, she'd go to the police station herself.

Darla climbed out of the cabinet and made her way down the darkened hallway to the offices.

Her heart raced just at the thought of going to the police. Darla had been picked up a time or two for prostitution until she'd found Jimmy. He'd protected her. Gotten her out of that. Made sure she had what she needed.

She laughed to herself. Now that he was gone, she was too damned old to go back to prostitution as an option. But that didn't mean the police didn't still freak her out. She would go to the police station this time, though.

She owed Jimmy that.

She opened the door to the office she'd seen Jimmy come out of twice when they'd come to the clinic to pick up his meds. She didn't have a flashlight and turning on the lights wasn't an option.

"Damn," she muttered. She shoulda thought of that. She made her way to the desk and felt around. A bit of light came into the room through the slats in the shades, and her eyes were adjusting to the dark.

She turned toward one wall that looked to have filing cabinets standing against it. Would they keep files documenting what they were doing? She didn't know, and she wasn't sure how she'd even read them in this dark, but she moved toward them. Maybe she could grab a handful of them and go out into the hallway where the lights had been left on and read them there?

She saw the movement right before she felt the pain in the side of her head. Stars exploded as she went down and she hit her chin on the corner of the desk. Pain radiated through her jaw as her teeth clacked together in a ferocious snap. She looked up and saw a man lean over her. He was nothing more than a shadow, but he was tall. His silhouette was the last thing she saw before he kicked her in the head. Once, twice. She gasped at the pain and fought to keep her eyes open, but darkness closed over her and she was powerless to fight it.

CHAPTER 29

HE HUNG UP THE PHONE. This was the last thing he needed now. He'd sent Sykes over to the clinic last night to tie up loose ends, not make more of them.

What the hell had Sykes been thinking grabbing the woman? He sent a few texts to get the right people lined up and everything in place for cleanup. Ten steps ahead had included lining up the paid muscle he would need for this job, too.

Ten steps ahead always paid off.

One last text to Sykes. *Leave her at the factory and get to the cabin. I'll meet you there tomorrow.*

He didn't wait for a response before dialing Coleman.

"Meet me in twenty minutes." He hadn't bothered to tell Coleman who it was. The man would know.

"What? I can't just leave the clinic any time you call."

"I'm heading to the factory now, Coleman. If you're not there, I'll have the man I've got following your wife and daughter bring them to me instead."

A string of curses came through the line and he felt a flash of remorse for bringing the daughter into things. Only a flash, though. He didn't regret what was going to happen to Coleman, although perhaps he should have. The doctor really was nothing more than collateral damage. But Coleman had brought this on himself with his gambling.

If Coleman truly loved his family, if he really was a good father to his daughter, he wouldn't have leveraged everything he had for the high he got from gambling. A father should be stronger than that.

He tuned back in to Coleman's useless rant. "You son of a bitch. I swear to God, if you touch one hair on her head—"

"The factory, Coleman. I'll see you at the factory."

Coleman was stupid enough to believe he'd actually be there. The doctor would never see it coming.

* * *

Mia gripped the steering wheel tightly as she watched the clinic, then glanced at the dashboard as her phone buzzed in its holder.

Sorry, meeting ran over. Be there in fifteen. Wait for me!

She'd taken a half day at work and Jax was meeting her so they could try talking to Dr. Coleman directly. She wanted to look in the doctor's eyes as she asked how her father had died and see for herself if he was involved in whatever was going on. She needed to know.

She and Jax had argued over whether it was a good idea. She'd finally won the argument when she'd said Jax could come with her and they'd confront the doctor at the clinic. Even Jax had to agree that was safe. Besides, Dr. Coleman didn't seem dangerous. If anything, he might be the weak link who could be pressured to open up and tell them what was going on. If he was giving people experimental drugs that were leading to their deaths, it would go against everything he'd sworn to when taking the Hippocratic Oath. It went against everything a doctor stood for.

There was simply no way the doctor could be doing this on his own. He had to have some company providing a test drug. Not to mention they'd need to have some plan for how they'd get this drug approved.

That was one thing Mia didn't understand. "How do they plan to get the drug approved someday? It's not like they could go to the FDA and say here's this data from this fake test we did. This illegal fake test. They can't do that, so what's the point? What's the end game here?"

She had no idea who *they* were, but talking about the issues out loud helped her work through them.

She looked at the locks on her doors again. She'd been checking them obsessively every few minutes. She was locked in. No one could get to her in her car. As long as she waited for Jax, she was safe.

Mia eyed the time. Another ten minutes until Jax would arrive. She swallowed hard, planning what she would say when they were able to get in to see the doctor.

A man came storming out of the building, looking over his shoulder as he walked to the parking lot, then dialed his phone. She was too far away to hear, but he was yelling something, and his face was filled with rage. She knew from his picture on the clinic marketing and fundraising materials that he was Dr. Coleman. That was the man she'd come to confront.

And he was about to drive away.

Mia bit her lip, looking at the time again. At least five minutes before Jax would arrive, and something told her she needed to see where the doctor was headed in such a hurry.

"Why would he leave in the middle of a work day?"

Biting her lip, Mia started her own car as he pulled out

of the parking lot and fell in a few cars behind him.

"What are you doing, Mia?" She asked herself.

She would text Jax when the doctor stopped and let him know where to meet her. Whatever was happening didn't add up. The doctor wasn't acting the way she expected a doctor to act. It was a Friday afternoon. He should be in the office seeing patients, not running out of the building and speeding down the street.

She followed several cars behind, heading straight through neighborhoods that were seeing the early stages of gentrification. They entered areas that hadn't seen even the early stages of that process, and Mia thought of turning around. This wasn't safe. But she'd grown up in some areas that were less than safe. She could handle herself. Or at least fake her way out of a situation with tough talk and bluffing. Maybe.

The doctor pulled into the old Smythe Repeating Arms Company building. It was actually a series of four buildings that took up a four block radius and had been empty for well over a decade. The few houses around it looked like they might fall down with a simple gust of wind and she knew they must have been condemned. She had heard something about a plan to tear the entire area down and build an apartment complex with restaurants, a park for children, and a small grocery store, but that hadn't happened yet.

Mia circled around the block and back to where the doctor's car was parked. A flash of the white shirt the doctor was wearing told her he'd just entered one of the old buildings. She pulled over on the street and parked, then texted Jax.

Followed Dr. Coleman to Smythe Arms Bldg. Come there?

CHAPTER 30

"REALLY? THAT'S HIM?" Cal looked over Jarrod's shoulder at the computer screen.

"Not what I expected, either." Jarrod had thought Warrick Staunton would be a lot older than the man in the photo. "He's what? Thirty, if that?"

Cal shrugged. "Maybe he looks younger than he is. It's a family company, right?"

"Yeah. Started by this Staunton's great uncle on his mother's side. That's where the name Simms comes in. Her maiden name is Simms."

"Who's this guy?" Cal pointed at another name along the left hand side of the screen where the menu showed company profiles. "Jonathan Simms? Carissa Hastings mentioned a Jonathan, too, when Jax heard her on the phone, right?"

"Yeah," Jarrod looked down at his notes. "No last name, but this could be him." He clicked the link and the face of a man in his fifties filled the screen. The men were quiet as they skimmed the bio. Simms was Warrick Staunton's uncle, and a researcher in the company.

"I wonder why he isn't running the place?" Cal asked absently as Jarrod printed photos and company information.

Cal grabbed the stack of printouts and tossed them on his desk. "I've found several other companies that fund the shelter or the clinic. Simms is one of the heavy hitters, for sure, but Branson Medical and Tyvek Technologies donate a big chunk of money, too."

Cal shuffled through the papers lining the side of his desk. He wasn't nearly as neat as Jarrod. Jarrod believed in file folders and drawers. Cal was one of those people who swore he knew where everything was even if there was no rhyme or reason to it all. "Here it is."

He pulled out a sheet and handed it to Jarrod. "Tyvek Technologies and The Victoria Tyvek Staunton Memorial Foundation are the other two big donors."

Jarrod raised a brow. "*Victoria Tyvek Staunton*? Any relation to Warrick Staunton?"

Cal nodded. "Wife. She died in a car accident three years ago."

"Wow." Jarrod clicked the back button on his browser, looking at Warrick Staunton's photo again. "This guy's a widower?"

"Yeah. Like I said, maybe he's older than he looks. She was high on all kinds of pain pills and shit when she died."

Jarrod shook his head. They'd seen that shit all too often.

"And get this, her dad is William Tyvek."

Jarrod glanced at the pages Cal had given him moments before. "As in Tyvek Technologies?"

"Yup. That guy. Started the company and built it from nothing. She was his only daughter. Apparently, he raised her on his own after the mom died of cancer when she was a little girl."

Jarrod raised a brow at Cal, who simply shrugged in return. "It was in the articles I read. Sad story."

Jarrod agreed, but he wasn't going to sit here and hash it out like some soap opera. "So, that means Tyvek Technologies, the memorial fund, and Simms Pharmaceutical are all linked? And *all* of them are major funders for the clinic?" Jarrod shook his head.

"I'm not sure if Branson Medical is tied into them somehow or not." Cal lowered his frame into the ancient chair in front of his desk and leaned back.

"Jax overheard Carrie Hastings talking to Staunton. He said Jonathan and the CEO of Branson Medical were friends. It's a loose connection, but it's enough to keep them on our list of people to look at in my book."

"Agreed," Cal said, with a nod. "I'll find out who the major players at Branson are. See if that leads us anywhere else."

✱ ✱ ✱

Mia watched as the doctor walked into the old factory complex. She checked her door locks once again and glanced around. The area was abandoned. Apparently, the rumors about development taking place here either weren't true, or the development wouldn't be happening for a while.

She looked at her phone again and put it on vibrate. She wanted to wait for Jax, but she also didn't want to lose track of where the doctor was. Slipping her phone in her back pocket, she unlocked the doors and crossed the street, her head on a swivel checking behind her the whole time.

Her dad had been taken away due to a series of horrible events. In her mind at that moment, everything was building up inside her, screaming at her to seek justice for a man who'd lost his wife and children. She'd lost not only her father but a brother she'd never have the chance to know. Her mother had lost her husband and son.

Her father had lost everything.

The thought that this doctor might have taken her dad away just when they'd had a shot at somehow having a relationship again fueled her anger and her actions.

She slipped into the complex, looking around at the rusted fire escapes and the broken windows.

What the hell is the doctor doing here? For once, she didn't voice the words aloud. She didn't make a sound as she pressed herself against one of the buildings and waited, watching the door the doctor had gone through.

She took out her phone again and checked the screen. No texts. No calls.

Mia heard shouting. Dr. Coleman was fighting with someone. Damn. She looked at her phone again and moved closer to the door he'd gone through. She could hear the shouting.

Need to hurry. Doctor arguing with someone.

She tapped the message out, then stood and waited. She shifted on her feet, checking over her shoulder again. This was stupid. She needed to get back to her car with its locked doors. She was safe there. If anyone came at her, she could drive away and get to help.

She turned to walk back, but stopped. There was still the sound of the raised, angry voices, but there was something else as well. Someone crying out. Muffled, as though the person's face or mouth was blocked, but definitely there.

Mia strained to hear it. The sound was gone. She'd imagined it.

She turned again, before spinning back.

"I didn't imagine that," she said to herself, almost a whisper.

Her phone pinged a text alert.

Wait for me! Wait!

Mia switched her phone to silent and looked back toward the building. She couldn't ignore those cries. She just couldn't.

She entered the building the same way she'd seen the doctor go, and carefully made her way up a flight of stairs toward the sound of shouting.

No. When she got near enough, she could tell it was more than just shouting. There was a physical fight going on now, too. The sound of flesh and bone being hit reverberated through her ears. It sickened her and she turned to run, but heard the crying once again.

A woman crying. No doubt about it.

She cursed under her breath. This was crazy. Her memory of being attacked came back to her and she thought she might be sick as her whole body seemed to tense for flight. She needed to run. To get out of here and get help. But how could she when she had no doubt in her mind someone was in trouble there?

Mia followed the stifled sounds down several doors. "Stupid, stupid, stupid." She was that stupid girl in the horror movie. The one you couldn't help yell at.

She turned the doorknob on the room it was coming from as quietly as she could. Indecision and fear tore at her, but she couldn't leave. Not without trying to help.

There were still voices coming from the other end of the hall, but they weren't raised now. Whoever was fighting in there, they seemed to have stopped for the moment. As though one had won the fight and now held the fate of the other in their hands.

The thought sent a chill through her.

She opened the door and looked inside.

"Oh God." Mia rushed forward, dropping to her knees. "Darla," she whispered as her hands tore at the tape on the woman's ankles first. It was duct tape. She couldn't get it to tear in anything other than thin strips.

Mia looked around as Darla began to whimper. She had a large gash on the side of her head that was oozing thick blood at a slow pace. There was dried blood on her shirt, as though the wound had bled more profusely at some point, and dried over time. Her face was swollen and bruised, and one eye was nearly shut.

"Shh. You have to be quiet, Darla. They're close by. Just let me find something to cut this with." Mia crawled to the other side of the small closet that was Darla's prison.

She found an overturned bucket, a few rags, and empty boxes. Whatever this closet had once held had been rifled through and pilfered a long time ago.

A rusted piece of one of the metal shelves held the most promise. She picked it up and turned it over in her hands, hoping the slightly sharp corner on one side might be enough.

It seemed to take hours as she cut through the tape, bit by bit. Her hands slipped several times as her heart raced and sweat beaded on her face. When Darla's ankles were free, Mia turned to the tape on her hands. The last to go was the tape across her mouth, which Mia pulled off in one fast swipe of her hand. Darla grunted but kept her lips pressed together to silence herself as she brought her hands up to her face and covered the stinging skin.

Mia whispered. "The stairs are at the end of the hall. Can you walk?"

"I'm not sure."

Mia draped her arm under the other woman's arms to help give her leverage and lift her to stand.

"I've been here all night," Darla said, limping forward in a slow shuffle.

"We don't have time." Mia could hear the panic in her voice, but she knew they had only minutes to get out of the building. Something about the way the men had been fighting told her this was about to be a very bad place to be.

She moved awkwardly to the door, with Darla leaning heavily on her.

"I'm sorry. Body's half asleep."

"Listen Darla," she whispered, "we have to move now. Lean on me. We need to make it to the stairwell at the end of the hall."

Mia held her breath as they moved. The room where the men had been fighting was all too quiet now and fear like she'd never known flooded her body.

Twenty more feet. She focused on the stairwell, Darla's weight too much for her to hold.

A shout behind her. Dr. Coleman.

Mia looked toward the stairwell and focused on getting them to the door. They weren't going to make it.

CHAPTER 31

THE SOUND of the gunshot was enough to make Mia jump and she lost her hold on Darla.

"This way." Darla tugged at Mia's hand and pulled her into a room. She was walking better now and Mia hoped that meant the circulation was coming back into her legs. Either that or adrenaline was pushing the woman onward regardless of her condition.

Darla shut the door behind her and pushed a chair under the door knob. Broken abandoned furniture littered the room.

"The fire escape." Darla pointed as if she'd been in this building before and Mia realized it was probably a place where homeless people could get out of the elements at night or during cold weather.

Mia didn't like Darla's plan at all. She'd seen the state of the fire escapes on the old building when she'd come in. Rust covered the metal and she wouldn't be at all surprised to find gaps in the steps. She looked over her shoulder as they heard a man curse loudly.

She had a feeling Darla's captor had just discovered she was gone.

The two women went out the window, Darla leading the way. Mia tried not to look down. They were only four stories off the ground. If she didn't look down, just put one foot in front of the other, she could make it.

God, she hoped Jax was on his way. This was the dumbest thing she'd ever done. Hands down.

Then again, if she hadn't done it, she had a feeling Darla would be dead. She didn't know yet why that man had Darla or what his plans were for her, but a woman trussed up in an abandoned building was never a good thing.

Rusted metal cut into her hands as she clenched the stair rail, and her stomach swirled. They were almost at the bottom, where they'd have to go down the last bit on a ladder.

Neither woman talked, but it seemed to Mia that their breathing would give them away. It sounded so loud in her ears. Surely Darla's captor could hear them and know exactly where they were.

The door to the building flew open and a large man came barreling out of it. He looked around wildly as Mia and Darla froze, not daring to breathe. Her heart felt like it would break through the wall of her chest at any moment. They were sitting ducks if he looked up.

Mia held tight to the railing trying to make herself as small as possible. Trying not to move.

In the end it didn't matter that they didn't move. The man scanned the courtyard in all directions, before looking up. As he raised his gun, Mia shouted.

"Up Darla! Up!" She began to climb, straining to move faster and faster. A shot rent the air and something hit the metal next to Mia. Her arm stung, as though she'd been bitten by something much stronger than a mosquito, but her legs continued to churn. She stumbled and fell on the steps, but righted herself and kept moving. She could hear Darla behind her, but the woman was falling behind.

Mia turned back, grabbing at Darla's jacket to try to pull the woman along with her. Shots continued, but she wasn't able to tell how close they were coming. The man seemed to be firing wildly and all she could pray for was that he was a bad shot.

Would the police even come if shots were reported in this area? Would it matter?

The police couldn't possibly arrive in time to help them.

Mia saw movement out of the corner of her eye. Jax.

She didn't have time to process the wave of relief that hit her at the same time that dread hit. She was both relieved he was there, but also now more fearful for his safety than for her own.

Jax flew at the gunman, taking them both down to the ground. Mia screamed. She watched in horror as the two men grappled on the ground.

Jax had the gunman's arm and looked like he was trying to break it as the man struggled to hold onto the weapon.

Jax was on top, but the other man was so much bigger than him. So much that it scared the daylights out of Mia. The man's movements were awkward and clumsy, but sheer size gave him the advantage.

"Stay here," Mia said to Darla as she started back down the ladder. She had to do something. She couldn't just stand by and watch Jax get hurt. Or worse.

The gunman let out a scream that could only be caused by pain and Mia saw the gun fly from his hand. Jax hit him and the crack of bone reverberating through the air was a sickening sound she knew would never leave her.

The gunman recovered too quickly, as she scrambled down the steps, finally getting to the ladder part of the fire escape. She'd forgotten to be frightened of the rusted steps and the height. She saw only Jax as the tides turned and the large man began to strike back with giant meaty hands.

She knew those hands. They'd pinned her to the ground, struck her. This was the man who'd attacked her. Her hands shook, but she moved forward.

Jax lost his footing as the larger man rolled, punching Jax again and again. Mia felt sick.

She all but slid down the last rungs of the ladder, before dropping to the ground. She looked frantically around for the gun.

There.

She picked it up but realized she couldn't shoot at them. She had no idea how to fire a gun, and she was a lot more likely to hit Jax than she was to hit the other man.

Jax rolled the two again, hitting back as the other man went down.

Mia looked around the courtyard. It was strewn with garbage and junk.

She hefted a large piece of metal that looked like it had once belonged to the fire escape. How that thing had held her and Darla, she would never know.

Mia cursed as she realized she couldn't heft the weight of the bar without putting down the gun. There wasn't time to think the options through. She gave up the gun for the bar and came around behind the two men.

Jax was on top of the gunman. He yelled something to Mia but she didn't know what.

The gunman kicked out from under Jax. Mia watched

in horror as he dove for her, grabbing her before she could swing the metal bar.

He had her around the throat and was moving with her suspended like a rag doll before she knew what had happened. Pain shot through her neck and shoulder.

The gunman stopped, hitting a dead end where he'd corralled himself in the courtyard with no way to get to any of the exits.

She felt his hot breath close to her ear and a violent tremor raced through her as she remembered being pinned to the ground beneath him. Remembered his tongue on her face.

"I think I'll take you with me this time, baby," he said, nuzzling at her neck. His face was rough with stubble and she wanted to shove him away, but it was all she could do to stand on her tip toes and keep her airway open.

"Let her go," Jax said, an eerie calm to his tone as he squared off with the gunman. Time seemed to slow and the courtyard grew silent, save for the blood rushing in her head and the battered breathing of the man holding her hostage.

Jax leaned over and picked up the metal bar she'd dropped, moving slowly closer to her and her captor. The gunman was backed up against the building and Mia could hear the faint sound of sirens in the distance. Too far in the distance.

His grip on her throat tightened and her vision blurred. He lifted her higher and she dug her nails deeper into his skin, clinging to his forearms as her toes kicked for the ground. She gave up trying to reach the ground and kicked at her attacker's legs but her kicks were weak. It took all her strength to hold on to the man's arm in an effort to hold herself up.

It was an effort that was failing.

Her eyes were locked onto Jax's calm gaze as a garbled sound came from somewhere. No, not somewhere. It came from her as her body screamed for oxygen, crying out.

"Let her go," Jax said again, but the words were almost a growl. He was favoring his left leg and she could see he was slightly off balance, but he moved steadily toward the man holding her.

With a start, Mia realized she could make the gunman more off balance than Jax. She locked eyes with Jax and tried to communicate with him, looking from his face to the ground again and again.

Did she imagine the slight nod of his head? Had he dipped his chin on purpose because he understood?

It didn't matter. The grip on her throat was closing, tightening. The pain was nearly blinding. The panic suffocating.

It was desperation that caused her to act. She dropped her arms and let all her weight hang in a single motion. The man cursed and dropped her. Jax swung, a nauseating crack sounding as the man dropped on top of Mia.

* * *

"Mia! Mia!" Jax ignored the pain sluicing up his residual limb and through to his hip as he pulled at the dead weight on top of Mia.

Blood flowed from a cut in the man's head, but Jax didn't care. He just wanted to get Mia away from him.

Darla came up beside him. "The police are close," she said panting in rough gasps that would have worried Jax if he hadn't had all of his focus on Mia for the moment. Darla went around behind the gunman and shoved as Jax pulled. They rolled the unconscious man to the side, freeing Mia.

She lay still on the ground. Too damned still.

"No, baby. Please." Jax prayed like he'd never prayed before. Not even when he was overseas. The sight of Mia lying so limp and pale made his chest go tight. She was here because he'd pushed and pushed, insisting something had happened to Leo. If it wasn't for him, she wouldn't be hurt.

He heard more than saw police vehicles pull into the space and hoped it was Jarrod responding to his message.

"Mia." Training kicked in more slowly than he'd like it to. He put his hand to her neck. Her pulse was strong and steady. Airways clear. She was breathing. He ran his fingers along her neck and shoulders, checking for breaks. "Mia, wake up, sweetheart."

Uniformed officers entered the courtyard, coming at them, weapons drawn. Jarrod shouted instructions as the officers narrowed in on the gunman. Jax was never happier to see the detective.

"Ambulance, Jarrod." Jax called out. "She needs to get to the hospital."

"Two minutes out," was Jarrod's response.

As he looked back to Mia, ready to check her vitals, her eyes opened. She looked stunned, but zeroed in on him right away.

"Stay still," he said as he brushed the hair from her face. "There's an ambulance coming. You're safe." He pulled off his shirt and pressed it to her arm where blood flowed from a rough gash. He saw pain grip her as he pressed and tears fell from her eyes.

"I'd like it better if you'd just hold me." She whispered hoarsely, and he smiled at her sass in the face of all she must be feeling.

"I'll hold you plenty as soon as we get you checked out." He realized he was running his hands down her arms, her legs, over and over. He was checking. He couldn't stop himself if he tried. He needed to see for himself that she was okay. Needed it on a primal caveman level that shocked him.

"Promise?" She said and there was fear and uncertainty in her question that made his heart ache.

"Promise. You'll be sick of me in no time," he said as the EMTs moved in, pushing him to the side. He didn't go far, moving to be by her head as they worked. "I'm right here, Mia," he told her again and again. "I'm not going anywhere."

And he wasn't. Not for a good long while. Not forever, if she'd have him.

CHAPTER 32

JAX HELPED Mia through the front door of her house. "Do you need something to drink? Maybe something to eat?"

"Let the girl take a breath, Jax," said her mom, coming in behind them. There was an indulgent smile to her face that said she was enjoying chastising him.

"Sorry." Jax didn't let go of Mia's arm as he lowered her to the couch. Her ankle was wrapped and her throat was marred with the evidence of the gunman's hand around it.

He'd been identified as Trace Jones or Triple K, as he was apparently called on the streets. He had a criminal record a mile long, had been arrested for assault and the police suspected he'd been involved in at least one murder. He'd only had two assault convictions stick, but from what Jarrod had told them, that was only because he seemed to be good at wriggling off the hook.

He'd do anything that was asked of him for the right amount of money. They didn't know what his connection was to the clinic or Dr. Coleman yet. Both men had been rushed to the hospital in critical condition.

"You're just as hurt as I am." Mia pulled Jax's thoughts back to the present. "Sit."

He sat next to her as her mom went to the kitchen to get them both food and something to drink.

"You still need to tell me what you were thinking following that man there," Jax said, lowering his voice so her mom wouldn't hear.

It didn't work. Her mom must have had crazy-good ears. "Yes, she does!" She called out from the other room. "There's no excuse for that, Mia!"

Mia looked at him but shook her head. "If I hadn't gone, Darla would have died."

She wasn't taking any crap about her decision, and Jax didn't know if he should be proud or furious. He blew out a breath. He couldn't argue with the fact, but his gut still clenched at the thought of Mia in the hands of that man.

They were still waiting to hear if Dr. Coleman was going to make it through surgery.

Jax had seen the shock and confusion on the face of the doctor's wife when she and his daughter came into the waiting room. He had a feeling that whatever the doctor was involved in was going to come as a complete surprise to his wife.

"I don't know what I would have done ..." He stopped talking, mostly because he couldn't go on. He rested his forehead on Mia's and just focused on breathing without losing his shit.

He raised his head when he was sure he could speak. "I need you to know what you mean to me. What you make me feel. You're amazing, Mia. You're funny and kind. You risked your life to save Darla when no one would have blamed you for turning and running instead of getting her out of there. If that weren't enough, you manage to make me feel like a superhero with just a smile. If I'd lost you ..."

She placed a hand over his chest and laid her head on his shoulder. "Right back atchya."

He laughed and pulled her closer, if that was possible.

"Enough with the superhero crap. You two need to tell me why my daughter was almost killed," said Lynn coming in from the kitchen. Jax had forgotten they weren't alone and he cleared his throat and shifted so he wasn't quite so wrapped around Mia in front of her mom.

Before they could fill Lynn in, Jax's phone rang. Seeing it was Jarrod, he put it on speaker and set it on the table in front of him.

"Hey Jarrod. Mia and her mom are here, too."

"Hi guys. I'm afraid I don't have good news. Dr. Coleman just died on the operating table."

"And Jones still claims he doesn't know anything?" Jax asked.

"No. I'm afraid I'm beginning to believe him. His story is backed up by emails and he was paid in cash dropped at a bus station locker. We're working on tracing the emails he was sent, but the IP address comes back to a public computer at the library downtown."

"You can't track it?" Jax asked.

"We cross-checked library usage. You have to have a library card to use the computers. There's one card that was used during the time when each of the four emails he received were sent, but it comes back to a middle school kid who says he lost his library card a month ago and hasn't replaced it."

"Video?" Jax asked.

"No. The library doesn't have security footage. We

found footage of the cash drop at the bus station. All we've got is a tall thin man in a baseball cap and hoodie. Can't make anything out. Prints are useless in a place like a bus station, but we'll have crime scene check the locker and the bag the money was in just in case. Don't hold your breath on that one."

"So all there is to go on is tall and thin?" Lynn said, echoing the thought they were likely all having. "That could be anyone."

"We've interviewed the staff and nurses at the clinic. There are two doctors at the clinic who fit that description but both of them have alibies for that time frame. I did get permission from two of the other decedent's next-of-kin to test the tissue and blood samples, so the ME is running that now, but that's going to take some time. With Dr. Coleman's death, Darla's kidnapping, and the assault on Mia, we now have an official investigation open so we were able to get warrants to run tests on the samples from the unclaimed victims. I'm afraid that's the best lead we've got for now.

The clinic is cooperating as far as they're able. They're opening up all their records, except for the ones that involve drug trials run there, but they are legally obligated to wait for a warrant on that. We should have one by the end of the day."

Jax cursed under his breath. "Let us know what you find out?"

"As much as I can." Jarrod and Jax said the line together, a wry smile on Jax's face. He knew the detective couldn't share everything with them. They were lucky to be getting the information they were.

"Listen, I need to tell you both," Jarrod said, "it looks like Trace Jones isn't going to make it."

Jax froze. "What do you mean?" His mind ran back to the scene at the factory. He'd swung the bar hard at the gunman's head, but was it really *that* hard?

Jax met Mia's gaze as Jarrod spoke. "Sometimes it only takes one hit to the head. They're hoping to reduce the swelling and operate, but ..."

"What does that mean for Jax and Mia?" Lynn asked.

"It means we need you to come in sooner rather than later to give your statements. The district attorney wants to see the interview. He needs to make some decisions."

"Are you serious?" Mia stood and, even through her hoarseness, her tone was indignant, but there was a protectiveness there as well. Jax took hold of her hand and tugged her back down on the couch.

"I think it's just going to be a matter of procedure, guys," Jarrod said. "Just an issue of getting both of your statements on the record."

"These guys are exhausted," Lynn said.

"It'll hold until tomorrow. Come into the station in the morning and I'll get everything on the record."

"Thank you, Jarrod."

"You bet. Get some rest you guys."

Lynn looked from Jax to Mia and back again. "All right, never mind the district attorney. It's time for me to get the whole story. Spill it."

Mia sighed and Jax launched into the story, beginning with the break in at Leo's and skimming over the part where Mia was attacked and almost killed.

Lynn's facial expression stayed stock still while she listened to the story, but when it was over she came over and hugged Jax.

"Thank you," she said, pulling back and looking him in the eye. She paused a minute before looking at Mia and raising a finger to point at her daughter. "And you! You're grounded."

CHAPTER 33

JAX WOKE BEFORE MIA. The morning was quiet and still, but his body stirred as he looked at her sleeping next to him. She lay naked, hair mussed. Her face was peaceful, save for the bruising on her chin and neck.

Jax had to tamp down the anger that rose when he thought of that man's hands around her neck. He was still struggling with the idea that he might have taken another man's life. He'd served in the military in conflict, so he'd seen his fair share of death. And, yes, he'd taken lives. Somehow, though, he'd separated himself from that and he never thought he'd be in that position again.

He had to remind himself that he'd had no choice. Trace Jones hadn't given him any. It had been a matter of Mia's life or Trace's.

Jax took a deep breath and let it out slowly as he focused on Mia, blocking out all other thought. He focused on the smoothness of Mia's skin as he ran his hand up her thigh and over her hip. She was like a balm to him, calming him instantly.

He kissed the soft curve of her shoulder and she stirred,

pressing into him as his body raged to life for her. Her eyes found his and he pulled her toward him, their legs entangling.

"I love waking up to you," he said and buried his head in the sweet spot between her shoulder and neck, making her moan in response. Those moans were something he would never get tired of hearing.

"The feeling is mutual," she whispered, her hand covering his cock as she squeezed, tormenting him. She rolled him over and slid on top of him as he cupped her breasts and tried to take in every last gorgeous bit of her. He'd never get tired of the sight of her above him like this.

He reached beside him in the bed stand for a condom and rolled it on before lifting her up.

As she took him in, he had to clench his teeth to keep from coming. He watched as her eyes heated and his breath caught at the way she made him feel.

She was his and he didn't plan on giving her up anytime soon.

When they lay wrapped together after their love making, he whispered to her again.

"I want to keep waking up with you."

"We live in two different cities."

"We do," he agreed. "For now, we can take turns on weekends. We don't need to rush to change that, but I want you to know that I want to build a life with you. I'm not going anywhere."

She traced a path on his chest with her fingers as he spoke, but her eyes met his when she answered. "I'm not going anywhere either." She'd been running away from people all her life. Not physically. But emotionally, and the result had been the same. She'd made sure she never opened herself to love.

She smiled and kissed him. "I love you. I don't know how that happened. Lord knows I tried not to," she said.

He responded with a laugh, but told her what he'd known for some time now.

"I love you, Mia Kent. Lord knows I didn't try very hard not to," he said with a grin as she shoved at him playfully.

EPILOGUE

JARROD STARED at the photos he'd lined up on his desk. There was one of Warrick Staunton, head of Simms Pharmaceutical, and his Uncle Jonathan Simms. The family resemblance was clear in the color of the eyes and shape of the face, even though Simms's hair showed some whitening with age.

Meredith Ball, head of Branson Medical, and Edward Ball, her husband and the researcher who'd invented a large number of the medical devices that had put the company on the map, were the next two photos. He had to be at least twenty-five years her senior, if not more, and Jarrod made a mental note to check on their relationship and see if she'd married him for money or her position in the company or what.

He slid William Tyvek's photo into position on the end of the row. Jarrod had looked him up. Tyvek's company was the largest, and Tyvek was known for his ruthless tactics in getting the company where it was today.

He shook his head as he looked at the photos. The truth

was, they had nothing but speculation about illegal drug trials. Not a whole lot of anything to go on. Right now, he still had no test results back from the medical examiner and nothing to tie them to the deaths of the homeless people, other than their connection to the shelter.

They'd gotten news this morning that Trace Jones was in a coma and likely wouldn't come out of it anytime soon, but the doctors also stressed they couldn't be sure with head injuries.

Mia and Jax had come in for their interviews this morning, and the district attorney had been satisfied. Their stories matched. They were waiting to see if the crime scene techs came up with anything on the scene that poked any holes in those stories, but if they didn't, the district attorney would officially close the inquiry without filing charges.

Coleman's office had held some pretty damning evidence. Files with the records of the trials he'd been performing and his notes on the different results from each patient involved.

They were working on tracking down the other patients involved to be sure they were all safe and hadn't been affected by the medication, but it would take time to figure out exactly what had happened and find all of the patients involved.

"Jarrod." Cal walked in and looked down at the photos, frustration lining his features as well. He'd been following up with Dr. Coleman's wife, although Jarrod knew his interview would be preliminary at best. The woman's husband had just been murdered. They wouldn't get much out of her right now.

"Did he wake up at all?"

Cal shook his head. "No. His wife claims to have no idea what he was involved in or why he would have gone to the factory. I'm pulling financials and phone records, but that'll take a few days. But I just got a call from the uniforms looking through Trace Jones's place. They found an envelope full of cash. It's got the clinic's logo on it. I sent it to the lab to see if we can get any prints off it. I'm hoping to tie it back to Dr. Coleman."

"So it could be Coleman that hired Jones? They fought and Jones killed Coleman? It's definitely possible."

Cal grinned and Jarrod wondered what Cal knew that he didn't. "They found a burner phone at Jones's. Its number matches the number we found on the burner phone in Coleman's office. The two men had talked. A lot."

Jarrod nodded. "Good." It felt damned good to have some of the questions answered. Some of the loose ends tied up. He looked over at his partner. "So, what, we think Coleman was doing this alone with only hired help?"

Cal didn't answer.

"I don't buy it," Jarrod said, even though his partner hadn't argued the point. "I don't believe the doctor was acting on his own."

Cal rubbed the back of his neck. "Hell, neither do I." He still sounded like he wanted it to be that way, like he was hoping for the nice clean outcome.

Jarrod continued. "He's not a scientist, for one thing. And even if he did come up with the drug by himself, where would he be manufacturing it? It doesn't add up."

Cal nodded. "I have a feeling whoever is behind this will go into hiding. Lay low for the time being. They've taken out a big loose end with Coleman."

Jarrod crossed his arms. "Man I wish we'd been able to talk to him before he died. I gotta think he would have given up everyone involved before he went."

"Yeah. What now?"

The two men looked at the photo lineup.

"Now we analyze every freaking fact we can dig up on these companies. I have a feeling our answer is in here somewhere," Jarrod said. It had to be.

* * *

Allan Sykes was getting tired of waiting. He'd been told to come to the cabin days ago, then nothing. Radio silence.

He walked up the wooden steps, arms laden with groceries. The cabin was nothing like what he remembered from his family's trips when he was young. They'd rented small, bare-bones places with nothing more than a main room, kitchenette and bathroom.

This place was nothing like that. It was a full-blown house. The only thing that made it qualify as a "cabin" was the fact that it was made of logs and located out in the woods.

He'd waited to go into town to the convenience store, living on the canned soup and stews in the walk-in pantry, but he gave up today. He wanted milk and eggs, toast. He wanted a beer to drink in the evening. If he was going to be stuck twiddling his damned thumbs waiting for his boss, he was damned sure going to put that back porch to good use.

They didn't have steaks at the convenience store. That would have to wait until he made it to the next town over. For now, the hot dogs, chips, and beer would have to do.

He hardly had time to process the sight of the man sitting in the chair when he walked into the kitchen. No words were exchanged before the black hole of a handgun's barrel was staring at him.

Confusion struck him as he fell to the floor and watched as blood pooled beneath him. He couldn't move. Couldn't speak. Couldn't stop the man when he stepped over him, carefully avoiding the spilled blood, and walked out.

* * *

To read Jarrod's story, click here for *Cut and Run,* the next book in the *Sutton Capital Intrigue Series*: http://loriryanromance.com/book/cut-and-run

ABOUT THE AUTHOR

Lori Ryan is a NY Times and USA Today bestselling author who writes romantic suspense, contemporary romance, and sports romance. She lives with an extremely understanding husband, three wonderful children, and two mostly-behaved dogs in Austin, Texas. It's a bit of a zoo, but she wouldn't change a thing.

Lori published her first novel in April of 2013 and hasn't looked back since then. She loves to connect with her readers.

For new release info and bonus content, join her newsletter at http://loriryanromance.com/lets-keep-touch/

Follow her on Facebook at
https://www.facebook.com/loriryanromance/
or Twitter at https://twitter.com/Loriryanauthor
or Instagram at
https://www.instagram.com/loriryanauthor/

Made in the USA
Las Vegas, NV
11 September 2021

30072782R00120